The Negotiator's Cross

Kenneth Dekleva

The Negotiator's Cross

Published through Amazon KDP

The Negotiator's Cross is a work of fiction. Names, characters, titles of characters, and incidents – with obvious historical references – are products of the author's imagination or are used fictitiously and are not to be construed as real. Any resemblance to actual events, titles, organizations, or persons – with some obvious historical exceptions – is entirely coincidental.

ISBN: 9798837196089 (Paperback Edition)

Praise for Kenneth Dekleva's
The Negotiator's Cross

"Imagine a fever dream of espionage and exotic foreign capitals, literary allusions, a kaleidoscope of colors, sights, sounds and lyrical passages akin to Gabriel García Márquez's finest prose, and you will only begin to approach the wonders of Dr. Ken Dekleva's *The Negotiator's Cross*. Dekleva, a noted forensic psychiatrist for the U.S. Intelligence Community, national security commentator, and multilingual polymath has created a psychic whirlwind which will not let you go until the very end. And then you may well ask yourself, what was that truck that just hit me?"
—James Lawler, retired senior CIA officer and author of *Living Lies* and *In the Twinkling of an Eye*

"As a psychiatrist specializing in spies for over 35 years, as you might guess, I am also addicted to espionage thriller novels. By now, I thought I had heard, seen, and read just about everything on the subject. Not true. In Dr. Ken Dekleva's new espionage thriller, *The Negotiator's Cross*, it turns out that the central character is Father Ishmael, "an ordinary, devout Catholic priest." I initially wondered how would I be able to relate to such an unlikely and unfamiliar character's point of view. To my surprise, Father Ishmael grew on me rather quickly as he was not as simple as he first appeared. I came to understand that his harrowing backstory partly explained why he hoped to simplify his life by changing to a second career—a simple parish priest. Did his chosen mid-life crisis solution actually simplify his life? No such luck. Precisely because his integrity was so visible to a cast of treacherous actors within the worlds of espionage and intelligence, time and again he was regarded as the only possible trustworthy intermediary to help fix almost impossible deadlocks. As a result, we witness as Father Ishmael gets recruited, often unwillingly, into a series of complex and dangerous situations. Only an author possessing Dr. Dekleva's rich professional experiences combined with his extensive postings living abroad, could have created such fascinating insider-wise, gritty, and life-threatening predicaments, which take place in vividly drawn exotic locales. Add to that a propulsive story line and now you know why I was fully captured by this gripping novel, forcing me to finish it without pause for a single break."

—David L. Charney, M.D.

"A captivating crime story that takes the reader on a world tour of late twentieth century history and geopolitics. The plot dives into the hidden world of espionage and subterfuge, in which Kenneth Dekleva's Father Ishmael character brings to mind memories of John le Carré's George Smiley and Charles McCarry's Paul Christopher. A reading adventure!"

—Daniel Levin, author of *Proof of Life: Twenty Days on the Hunt for a Missing Person in the Middle East*

"Ken Dekleva has used his wide experience in the intelligence and psychology communities to craft a completely new style of thriller. His main character, a Catholic priest, offers the reader an entirely different view into this genre. Ken knows this world and takes the reader on a journey into dangerous country—both physical and mental dangers await. A solid five-star read."

—JR Seeger, retired CIA officer and author of the MIKE4 series.

"Kenneth Dekleva's *The Negotiator's Cross* is the magical story of Father Ishmael, a priest with a dark past, who finds himself on a journey where his faith and faithlessness are tested by gangsters and spies in Russia and Mexico. The story speaks to the emotional wisdom of listening to one's heart while moving through a dangerous and uncertain world. Adventure, intrigue, and betrayal play out on a broad canvas in this elegantly written debut novel."

—Paul Vidich, bestselling author of
*The Matchmaker, The Mercenary, The Coldest Warrior,
The Good Assassin,* and *An Honorable Man.*

"Psychiatrist Ken Dekleva is one of the top profilers of world leaders, and his spot-on assessments have earned him global recognition. His work for agencies and departments of the US Government helps to fill *The Negotiator's Cross* with the level and combination of authenticity and high drama avid readers of espionage want. With characters undoubtedly drawn from the merging of people whom he's come to know professionally, Ken delivers a novel packed with suspense and tension which makes it hard to put the book down. Anyone who enjoys a great "read" will surely come to appreciate what he has delivered and thus welcome Ken as a top writer in the genre in the same league as Tom Clancy."

—David Percelay, Harvard Business School graduate
and a past Vice President of CBS News engaged as an
independent consultant by Fortune 100 companies
in the arena of security and intelligence.

Table of Contents

Prologue

The dream always began in the same manner. He was alone, standing on a street corner near El Angel, in the middle of downtown Mexico City. Waiting, praying, searching for a sign. He could smell the odors of the city, he could feel its energy, its pulsations, its sensibility. *El sabor*, the taste. What Eliot Weinberger, the famous translator and poet, called "karmic traces." He stood in the heat, beads of sweat dripping down his neck, his clerical collar, his cassock, even his sandals. The noise was impressive, millions of cars zipping around him at the roundabout, honking, people yelling. And he waited.

He had been left a voicemail on his cell phone, with instructions. The voice had been soft, a woman's, telling him to be there at noon, and to wait for a signal. But he had no clue as to the signal, or who would deliver the message. He had risen early, said his daily prayers, including the Rosary, and had washed, showered, and dressed in his sandals, brown cassock, and cleric's collar. He didn't shave, and his appearance favored a three-day growth. Back then he had been young and felt that a priest should be comfortable, fitting in with young people, the next generation. That was the spirit of Vatican II, and one embodied by the new Pope.

He counted cars, tried to count them all, read the license plates. Odd or even? That would indicate the day of the week, per the city's strict emissions regulations. He counted, one, two, three, all the way to a hundred. And then began again. As a child in America, he had lived near a farm, and counted passing train cars every morning before prayers and school.

He couldn't make out the hostage. He was young, an American, dressed in jeans, a guayabera, and sandals. What was he doing in Mexico City? Why? He didn't know. There were no signs, no answers. The hostage had a wife and a young child. The wife was Mexican, a beautiful woman with little makeup, long brown hair, and dark eyes. In the dream, she held her young child's hand, and smiled. Dreams are wishes or wish fulfillments—that's what his confessor had once told him.

He had counted 497 cars, when he suddenly found himself hooded, alone, in a darkened room. A man with a calm voice, an elderly gentleman, wearing a suit and speaking in Spanish, murmured softly to him. He quoted passages from the Bible, recited Psalms, including his favorite, Psalm 23. "The Lord is my shepherd, I shall not want" … then he switched to Psalm 27, "The Lord is my light and my salvation. Of whom should I be afraid?" When Father Ishmael tried to speak, he was mute, frightened. His interlocutor again spoke softly, telling him not to fear, but to wait. He gave him a glass of water, and departed. Only the darkness remained.

Days went by, no food, just water. The cell was a cool, dark place, but clean. There was a nightstand, with a Bible and a pitcher of water. His phone was gone. The interlocutor returned daily. He spoke slowly, reciting passages from the Bible. He recited poetry, the words of great poet Octavio Paz, from the poem "Sunstone:" "I travel along the edge of your thoughts, and my shadow falls from your white forehead."

"*Quien es?*," his interlocutor asked.

He replied, "Whom am I? What do you want from me?"

"Nothing at all, just the truth," replied the gentleman. "I do wish to know, what were you doing at El Angel? Whom were you waiting for? Why are you here? Who are you? I have your cell phone,

2

passport, and your ID card. You are a priest, right? What is a priest doing, standing in the middle of Mexico City, near el Angel? Please, think carefully, and answer me."

"I don't know anything."

The next moment brought a hard whack to his knee with the gentleman's cane. He screamed, dropping to the ground, writhing in pain. All he heard was the tap, tap, tap of the cane on the floor.

And then, the man's calm voice again: "Please tell me, now."

"Stop, stop, stop. Jesus Christ, please stop."

He later realized that the gentleman had left. He never saw him again, but smelled his cologne, and could feel and hear that soft, mellifluous voice like a brook or a shallow creek.

Next, the hostage appeared. The young American now wore a dark suit with a conservative tie. Double-breasted, buttoned nicely. His shoes were gleaming, and Father Ishmael could smell the polish. A nice smell, like a shoe store, or a barbershop from his youth, where his father had taken him as child, to listen to the laughter and tales of men. But the hostage never spoke.

His wife and child appeared next, weeping softly, and holding the hostage's hand. The hostage smiled. His wife's tears fell upon the floor of the room. She walked over to him, removed the hood. The water and Bible had vanished. She touched the hostage's face gently, then walked out the door, leaving him in the room, alone, in emptiness.

Father Ishmael woke up screaming, then weeping, then laughing, slapping himself on his legs, over and over. "He's alive, I'm alive! God is good. God is great."

Dreams are wishes. And I am alone, always alone, but yes, God is with me, Jesus is with me, always — *Jesus, siempre estas con migo.*

Mexico City

I remember my arrival in Mexico City. I had flown in at night, alone, with only one suitcase. A priest's life should be simple, even a Jesuit's. The pilot's landing announcement had come on the edge of the city, thirty minutes prior to landing. I remember looking out the window, and all I saw was a sea of lights, twinkling, shimmering. The city was so big! And alive. It never slept.

I came out of the terminal to a sea of taxicabs, many of them green and white Volkswagen Beetles. I had been advised to avoid them, as many were members of a kidnap and crime ring. Instead of 'Herbie the Love Bug,' people called them 'Herbie the Kidnap Bug.' I got into a radio taxi and arrived safely at my small, cheap hotel near downtown.

I, Father Ishmael, was sent to Mexico City by my diocese in San Antonio, to minister to the needs of the expatriate community. They assigned me to a tiny church near the city center and gave me a small studio apartment. It was clean, fresh, with flowers and a coffee pot. I love coffee, I like grinding the beans each morning, I adore the smell of the roasted beans, and the aroma of the brew. It, and my Rosary, helped start the day. Mexico is a land of lush fruits and vegetables. There are mangos, guava, and various nopales. Those too, started my day.

Like many great cities, Mexico City is meant to be savored, tasted, and experienced physically. I found myself feeling more physical, even sensual, with my senses on overload, as I explored its streets, cafés, parks, museums, and churches. My mentor at seminary had always said, "Every priest should know his city. Even a Jesuit." We Jesuits, are prone to book learning, to the Word, and tend towards a love of reason, faith, and rhetoric. But I must have something of the Franciscan in me, for I love to walk outdoors, in parks, to smell the trees, plants, and to hear the birds, or the chatter of squirrels; and in parks, other sounds, the barking of dogs, the laughter of children, the chatter of mothers, the tender words of lovers on a bench, and the silence of the widower, feeding the pigeons from a bench. The smell of cigarette smoke blending with the fragrance of bougainvillea. All that is lovely is a gift from God.

When I arrived, I had to start my little parish from scratch. I had a small rental space, and it took some time to fix up. I found some parishioners to help me. There was the retired, elderly woman, who wore a plain dress and a colorful scarf. Then there was a local nun, dressed in her black habit, who sang and smiled as she worked. We had the altar, the Sacristy, and the confessional. The pews, made of cherry, a bright red hue. Mexico was earth. Mexico was colors, *de colores*. And I had a statue of the Virgin of Guadalupe, whom I prayed to daily, for she embodied Mexico, its spirit, its faith, and its beauty. I always enjoyed visiting the Cathedral, especially on December 12th, when millions of pilgrims would arrive, making the half-mile walk to the chapel at the summit, some even crawling or pushed in their wheelchairs, or carried by loved ones, hoisted atop shoulders. Their faith was remarkable. People would come from all over Mexico, hundreds of miles away, by air, train, vehicle, or even on foot. A sea of faces, of colors, of humanity. Peasants in simple wear, sandals, sarapes, mixed in with the well-to-do, the latter wearing suits, fashionable dresses, Rolex watches, and the finest jewelry, their children in their Sunday best, and their bodyguards nearby, wearing dark suits, earpieces, and their guns, always their guns, never far away, always handy. Like a friend, a former undercover federal agent in Mexico said, "The gun always came out of the holster fast." That's how he survived.

I walked every day, often for miles, exploring the city. There was Chapultepec Park, with its games, taco stands, pinwheels, colors, artisans, and a gaggle of entertainers. And just caddy-corner, the Rufino Tamayo Museum. I was bewitched by its eerie quiet, vivid colors, and the paintings of howling wolves, dogs, animals. Visceral, in the flesh. Not in the spirit. And I would walk. Up the hill, through the pristine neighborhoods of Lomas Altas. Here lived the wealthy, politicians, businessmen, diplomats, and yes, even narcotraffickers. The houses had huge, lavish gardens, and exhibited the loveliest of styles, rapturous colors, and the smells of blossoms, shrubs, and trees. So much green and color, in a city of concrete. I came to know the streets of Polanco, with their stores, cafés, and restaurants. A bit too commercial for me at times, but I sometimes needed a good meal, aside from the neighborhood taco stand. I found a café that I enjoyed, where I'd converse with locals.

I'd also drive a few miles south, down to San Angel and Coyoacan. San Angel had beautiful, tree-lined streets, with a central plaza filled with musicians, street artists, and stores, all next to delightful cafés and restaurants, where the mariachis would serenade guests at lunch. I found myself walking, chatting with the street artists, and enjoying their talents, their gifts. As I say in my homilies, all persons have gifts and talents, given to us by God. For He is always with us. Coyoacan had similar qualities as San Angel. But its delight was the Frida Kahlo Museum. Outside, a blue house, filled with her furniture and art, and her vibrant, but later, damaged spirit. An artist of prodigious gifts, she knew and embraced suffering. She was so very Mexicana in this way. But she was terribly self-absorbed, constantly documenting herself in paintings, diaries, and photos. To understand her art, one had to embrace Frida, all of her. Her abandon, her passions, lovers, sexuality (yes, even her bisexuality), her sense of loss, her loneliness, and her pain. Her complex relationship with Diego Rivera and her love affair with the doomed exile Leon Trotsky, who would die at the hands of NKVD assassin Ramon Mercader, his skull split open by an ice axe.

I cannot say enough about the churches of Mexico, the great cathedrals. My favorites are the Cathedral of Guadalupe and the great, gothic cathedral in the center of San Miguel de Allende. Its spires and steeples aim skyward, as if perpetually seeking heaven.

But sometimes I needed quiet and peace, away from my little parish. Then I would drive to a small church designed by Luis Barragan. I found its serenity and its yellow, vivid colors nothing short of remarkable. I reveled in its emptiness. Sometimes a church should be experienced empty, like a vessel poured out. It is then that one comes close to God. *Jesus, bendiga me, siempre estés con migo.* I will never leave you.

My parish is mostly expats, a mixture of businesspeople, diplomats, well-off Mexican-Americans, and academics on sabbatical in Mexico City. All are fluent in Spanish, many staying for years or even decades, and many are married to a Mexican. There are many children. Like a Mexican ranch hand told a friend of mine in San Antonio, who desired grandchildren: "*Señor, si quieres nietos, tus hijos tengan que buscar unas esposas Mexicanas.*"

My Masses are bilingual. I give short homilies, often speaking of prudence, kindness, and faith. I love parables, for that is how Jesus taught us. I'm not much of an intellectual, although I enjoy books, most of all the greatest of books. Perhaps I am not as Jesuit as I think. I feel more like a Franciscan.

I grew up in San Antonio, the child of an American, Scots-Irish father, and a Mexican mother. My skin is thereby olive-colored, and I have dark eyes. I wear glasses, and am tall, with a priestly paunch. (What priest doesn't enjoy a few glasses of wine with dinner?) My family lives in Texas, and it's part of who I am. My childhood was one of faith, hard work, and being outdoors. My father owned a small ranch and farm in the Hill Country, and we'd spend weekends there, driving around and chasing errant calves, and branding cattle annually. We had Mexican ranch hands who taught me to ride, rope, and lasso a calf. In the evenings, they'd sit around a campfire, grilling steaks – tampiquena, with lime and cilantro – while singing *cumbias* and drinking tequila. My brothers and I felt at home. There was a sense of kinship and belonging. The ranch was ours, *nuestra communidad*. Summers would get hot, and we'd sit in the shade of an acacia tree, smoking, drinking guava juice, and waiting, watching, hoping to see the stars at night.

My father traveled a lot on business, and how I missed him. As a child, I'd sit outside on the front porch, waiting for him to return, watching for his car to pull up. I'd run to him, and embrace him, and he'd hold me tightly and reply, "I love you too, son."

I became a priest both by accident and calling. My mother taught me to pray, to pray the Rosary daily, and perhaps that planted the seeds of desire in me. I was an altar boy too. But I fought the calling, for it *is* a calling. The priesthood calls one, not the other way around. I came it to later, after serving in the military. I grew up ill-suited for school, preferring sports, action, rodeo, riding motorcycles, and chasing girls. When Uncle Sam called on me—Be All That You Can Be—well, that's how it began.

I was in a regular intelligence unit, doing a desk job, reading cables. Nothing special. One day, deliverance came. An NCO visited my unit and asked to chat with me.

"Let's have coffee. You like coffee, no?" Then he switched to Spanish. His *Espanol* was beautiful, like that of Octavio Paz, Carlos Fuentes, and Pedro Paramo. He found a quiet café, where we chatted. He knew all about my background, my family, my language test scores, my abilities in sports, and my outdoor skills. I had grown up hiking, riding horses, shooting guns, and performing in rodeo competitions. He had interviewed my friends, parents, siblings, neighbors, teachers, our family priest, and my other associates.

My childhood was never far away from me. For me, Texas was more than home. It had a history and sense of place, a way of being. It was all very physical. I remembered the heat of the summers, dozens of hundred-degree days, only to be cooled off by a summer thunderstorm, washing away everything in its sight. I cherished my memories of hiking in Caprock Canyons, awed by their majestic beauty, and knowing their blood-soaked history, where Comanches and the descendants of today's Texas Rangers had fought, and died. There too, one could see orange and blood-red sunsets for hundreds of miles on a clear day. And there, I could be alone, hiking for days without seeing a soul. That too, was Texas.

Who could not savor the summer rains in Mexico City? The rain would wash away the pollution and grime of the city's streets. It was purifying, cleansing. Like washing away our sins. It reminded me of summer thunderstorms in the Texas Hill Country. The skies would darken, their colors in the early evening, changing from blood-red to black, and winds, hail, and lightning would ensue. The flash floods were something to behold. They too, would wash everything away. And then it would be over, and at night you could see the stars again, forever and eternal. This too was Texas, God's Country.

I remembered hiking in Caprock Canyons once, and I came upon an elderly hermit. He was a Mexican, and we spoke in Spanish. He offered me water and asked, "*Hijo, conoces a Dios*?" "My Son, do you know Jesus?"

"Of course, Señor. He is always with me."

The hermit was dressed in a sarape, with loose-fitting pants. He lived in a small hut. We sat outside, and he offered me some brown tequila. It tasted awful. The hermit spoke of God, and how he saw Him every evening in the stars. His eyes sparkled as he spoke, but he smelled horribly, and his beard was long, stringy, and matted. He told me, "Without God, we are nothing."

I asked him, "How long have you lived here?"

He didn't really say. Rather, he spoke of eons, centuries, and of times past. He said, "My time ain't mine, it all belongs to God."

We parted ways, like two lost pilgrims.

The Spanish-speaking NCO had an offer. "We have a special, elite unit. It doesn't have a name. The training is very demanding.

You'll do small-arms training, martial arts, survival training, interrogation training, jump school, and surveillance detection. You'll get a private pilot's license. You won't exist and you will never wear a uniform. You will travel constantly, overseas, but I can't tell you where to."

I signed the form, and it all began. A year later, I had completed all of the required schools, at various bases and in other civilian locations across the country. My hair grew long, and I wore jeans and sandals to the office. I carried a 9mm automatic and, always, a switchblade. If you're in a fight rolling around on the ground, you've got to get to that knife fast, they taught me. Stab, cut, slice. Blood is good. Blood ain't water.

The training was brutal. And it was all done solo. They wanted to see if we could master our fears. They dropped me off in the middle of the Canyonlands in Utah for a week during the hottest part of the year, with a knife and no food or water. I had to arrive at Tucson a week later, clean-shaven and wearing a suit. I don't know how I survived. I lost thirty pounds. I ate bugs, tracked with the stars, and sipped water from desert sediments, tiny oases. I caught a rattlesnake, skinned it and cooked it. It tasted good, real protein. Coyotes followed me at night, waiting to kill; they howled, and I sang, cried out in fear, and howled back. Buzzards circled overhead. A mountain lion came within a few feet of me, sniffing my lair. I became like an animal…I became one of them. I spoke their language and didn't fear them. I relied upon my faith. They were God's creatures too. I was in Eden.

The martial arts training was particularly cruel. They taught me well, but for the final test, they blindfolded me and came at me with sticks, knives, whips, and chains. They beat me for two hours, screaming, "MOVE MOTHERFUCKER, keep moving! NEVER STOP MOVING! MOVE YOURSELF. BE FREE!" Somehow, I disarmed several of them, grabbed a knife and stick, and then it ended. Pain is a great teacher.

One of the instructors, a tough, stocky, somewhat fat guy, used to tell me, "Pain is just weakness. Hope is for the weak. Movement is better than hope." This teacher…he was tough. He was half-Mexican and had worked undercover for years along the border. The cartels had caught up with him, stabbed him, and thrown him in the Rio Grande, leaving him to die. He floated, barely conscious, until somebody pulled him out miles downstream.

When I arrived at the office I thought, *I made it, I'm done, I'm all in.*

Well, not so fast, hombre.

Without warning, I was arrested, hooded, beaten, and starved for three days. I was stripped naked, with only a dirty cloth covering. My interrogators spat on me, cursed me, called me a fucking wetback, and stuck my head in a filthy toilet. I vomited, pissed myself, and blacked out…. There's much I don't remember. I wondered, is this how Christ suffered for our sins? Must I too suffer as He did? I cried, wept, and bled. After three days, they left me alone with a piece of bread and a cup of water. Man does not live by bread alone, right? Then I was hallucinating, and my interrogators appeared, hugging me, weeping, pleading absolution, and kissing me. A female interrogator gently touched me face, caressing me like a child. They carried me to a warm bath, fed and clothed me, and so it went.

Finally, I was done. *Gracias, por Dios, Gracias a Dios, ayuda me por siempre, y siempre estés con migo.* The Lord is my shepherd, I shall not want.

Our military unit tracked bad guys, mostly narcotraffickers in Latin America. We stayed away from the embassies and traveled incognito on regular passports. We were on our own and had no diplomatic immunity if caught. We had to procure our own cars, motorcycles, weapons, radios, and surveillance gear. The latter was shipped through the embassies and then stored in our safe houses. We stayed in cheap shacks, apartments, and low-budget hotels. We recruited agents, and met with military officers, spies, diplomats, businessmen, clerks, prostitutes, and police officers. We met them in offices, homes, cafés, restaurants, bars, airports, discos, churches, parks, houses of ill repute, airport lounges, museums, and movie theaters. Many of the meetings took place at night. We changed our look constantly, and often wore disguises. My favorite was being a ranch hand because I had grown up around ranches in Texas. It felt natural. I could be whomever I wanted to be, just like in the Army.

I was very good at recruiting agents. While some were high-level contacts in the military, intelligence services, or law enforcement, others were of humbler stock. I remember one of my best informants, an elderly Mexican grandmother, a true abuelita. She'd refuse to talk until she had fed me her delicious, homemade tamales. She'd serve them with rice and a salad of nopalitos, then chain-smoke and sip on mescal. Her grandson was a trafficker. She had a head full of memories, of family gatherings, prayers, food, and fiestas. But she had other, more grim tales, of kidnapping, torture, and murder. She told me, "Son, you can't know the story in its entirety, without knowing me, and knowing Mexico. If you don't understand, then you're a fraud." She was also a healer and bruja. She too, was Mexico.

I loved the work, the mission, and the camaraderie. I totally drank the Kool-Aid, and soaked up the adrenaline rush of recruiting a narcotrafficker, or of turning their information over to the DEA or CIA, where they would handle them. But one day, several years later, something changed. It all happened so fast. I was in a military helicopter as an observer, flying with local police. There were flying an arrested trafficker to a different city, where he would be met by other authorities and undergo further interrogation. Suddenly one of the locals cursed at him, "Puta Madre," and shoved him out the helo door. I heard his screams every night for months. I went home on leave, and confessed my sins, but even that didn't help. I didn't feel absolved. One day I walked into the office, and said, "Guys, I can't do this anymore." I got discharged honorably and was back in Texas in 24 hours.

I didn't know what to do and felt deeply lost. One day I walked into a small church in San Antonio. I took confession, prayed the Rosary, and knelt quietly in a pew. I was the only person in the church. I started weeping softly, and only later did I feel a gentle hand on my shoulder, and a kind voice asking me in Spanish, "*Mi hijo, como puedo ayudarte a ti?*" The priest took me for coffee, and we talked for hours. He offered prayer, solace, and comfort. Like the famous martial artist Terry Dobson wrote years later, a kind word turneth away wrath. And so it went. A few months later, I found myself enrolled in seminary school in Texas.

The work in my small Mexico City parish brought me solace and joy. I preached, gave Holy Communion to the sick, presided over weddings, baptisms, and first Holy Communion. I knew my sheep, and they knew Me. It was enough, it felt just right. I felt human again, and Christ was always with me. It was a quiet simple life, a simple Christian existence. But God changes us in so many ways, and we are never fully cognizant of His Ways. If He said, Follow Me, I would go.

It started with a phone call. The American Ambassador's staff aide called me and said, "The Ambassador would like to have a courtesy visit with you. A driver will pick you up tomorrow." This was odd, as I didn't know anybody at the embassy, and had purposely stayed away from any official US government entities. My prior service record had been sanitized and, frankly, didn't exist. I had been in a unit that wasn't supposed to exist. Therefore, that part of me could not exist. For these reasons, I was puzzled and wondered what the Ambassador wanted.

I showed up the next morning, escorted to the Ambassador's plush office. We met alone, and he was kind and gracious, offering me coffee and chocolates as we sat. He started by asking about me but soon revealed that he knew about my past military service. It turned out that the Ambassador was, like me, part Mexican, and we spoke in Spanish. He was a classy person, a gentleman, who had worked for years in the media industry and advertising. He had been appointed by President George H.W. Bush, a personal friend. He wore a dark suit with a conservative tie. His cologne smelled nice. He looked dignified. But there was something unusual about him, and I couldn't put my finger on it.

He had a small request. "Could you come by weekly and give me Holy Communion? Because of my schedule and various security constraints, I often can't attend Mass locally. But participating in the Eucharist is important to me. I would be most grateful."

And so it began. He gave me his home phone number and a challenge coin, as well as a pen and keychain with his insignia.

Sometimes I wish I'd said, "No, thank you. I am so sorry, Mr. Ambassador, but I cannot accommodate this request." Yet something in the man's eyes and smile weakened my resolve, and I acquiesced.

He grasped my hands firmly and gave me an *abrazo*, like a true Mexican. "Thank you, Padre."

Deep Cover

Francisco didn't really exist. He had been in Mexico City for several years, working as a businessman for a small American trading company. He traveled a lot throughout Mexico, Central America, and Latin America. He had been to Havana twice, and to Haiti as well. Francisco worked for the CIA, as a deep-cover, non-official cover officer, known as a NOC. He had never been to the embassy, or to any American embassy for that matter, and had no diplomatic immunity. He was Mexican-American, spoke fluent Spanish, and had a wife (from Puerto Rico) and a young child. Francisco looked like a mestizo and dressed in a tan, conservative suit, with patent leather loafers, and an elegant tie from the Museo de Bellas Artes. He was a handsome fellow, and his wife was, well, drop-dead gorgeous. She looked like a movie star. Francisco liked art, music, a good cigar, and a nice scotch after work. He enjoyed reading and playing with his child or taking her to Chapultepec Park. Like many expats, he was Catholic and attended Mass downtown in the small parish attended to by Father Ishmael. They had become close, and Francisco's family had even hosted Father Ishmael over for dinner on many an occasion. Father Ishmael had celebrated their child's first Holy Communion.

Francisco had joined the agency straight out of business school in Miami, after working for a few years for a mortgage loan company and, later, a savings and loan institution. One day toward the end of his graduate studies, a recruiter had come by. He was a banker, very suave, dressed in a bespoke suit, with a wine-colored pocket handkerchief and a dark red tie. He wore Oxfords and had on a Rolex watch. Francisco couldn't place him, but he looked Spanish, and spoke with a Castilian accent. He looked like somebody out of *GQ*, except that he was in his mid-50s. He spoke softly and listened with intensity. His voice was like sipping a fine glass of Cabernet. His eyes were lucid and dark. It was odd. He looked like a banker, and dressed like one, but something didn't quite fit.

They ordered a nice lunch and, over wine, dessert, and cappuccino, the banker spoke. "Would you like to work for me, for a major international shipping company, based in Mexico City? Your home base would remain Miami, but your office would be in Mexico. You'd travel a lot and have regional responsibilities. You'll be dealing with a lot of major players and high net worth individuals. You're the right candidate for this job, and we've followed your career closely. Your clients at the mortgage loan office – many of whom are foreigners – adore you. Please let me know by next week. There will be some paperwork and approximately a year of specialized training, all here in Miami."

Francisco thought, *This is a weird job interview.* The banker left his card and number, but only gave his first name, Sergio.

When Francisco called the number the following day, he only got voicemail. Strange. But he thought, why not? His wife was willing to give it a go. Mexico City sounded exciting, so why not? *Por que, no?*

After he passed his background check, medical/psychological exams, and polygraph, he realized what he had gotten himself into. He couldn't tell anybody, not even his wife, best friends, or his family. Training took place in apartments and hotels in Florida. His teachers had all worked overseas, many for decades. Many were immigrants and spoke several languages fluently, even without an accent. He learned how to recruit an agent, how to spot surveillance, and how to start a new business. He drove a nice car, a cream-colored Mercedes. All of his computer and phone communications were above-board, and the most sensitive reports were to be given in-person in Miami (to Sergio) on a regular basis. He took lessons in defensive driving, and even took acting and improv classes to learn about his own emotions and how to express them. CIA had borrowed this methodology from the great KGB General Yuri Drozdov, the founder and director of the legendary 'illegals' directorate, who had himself, as a young illegal in Germany, studied acting under Berthold Brecht.

Francisco was trained to laugh, cry, and grow angry on demand. His CIA trainers told him, "We aren't teaching you how to use guns, or how to survive torture. You are *not* a spy. You are a businessman. Your body language, your psyche, your complete existence is that of a businessman. Guns, fast cars, chases, jumping off heights, rappelling, and martial arts—that's for others. Please take up lessons in golf and tennis. That's what businessmen do, OK?"

He nodded.

"Got it?"

"Yes."

What they didn't tell him was that if he got caught, he was on his own. He could be imprisoned, tortured, or worse. But by then Francisco had already figured that out.

The final exam was a bit of a challenge. They flew Francisco to Panama City and left him with an overnight bag, $200, and no passport. They told him, "Make friends. Use your creativity. See you in Miami in two weeks." And that's what he did. He stole a passport from a Canadian tourist, drove to Belize with a bunch of hippies and scuba divers, hung out there for a week, got drunk on tequila, and boarded a cruise ship back to Miami. He showed up at Sergio's Miami office wearing a seersucker suit, sporting a nice tan, and toting $20,000, which he had won gambling on the cruise with a bunch of Colombians, Mexicans, and Panamanians. "What a character, that gringo. A real fucking hombre."

Francisco didn't always recruit agents. But he was very good at spotting and assessing those targets who might be recruited. His job was to learn, to gather, and to listen. He might offer a kind word, reassurance, patience, and hope to a potential agent. He knew their fears and anxieties, and he never forgot a holiday, a birthday, or an anniversary; if one of his people fell ill, he would visit them, bringing medications, salves, balms, and ointments, like a shaman of sorts. He understood human vices. He understood sin, greed, larceny, and betrayal. And so, over the years, a bevy of Russian, Chinese, Cuban, and Venezuelan diplomats and intelligence officers, as well as narcotraffickers and corrupt businessmen, would find themselves being quietly approached by CIA and receiving an offer they couldn't refuse. None of them ever suspected Francisco. Matter of fact, over golf and drinks, several would complain to him about the aggressive approaches from the Americans. "*Que mala onda! Que barbaridad!*" And so forth.

It was a good life. They lived in a gorgeous home in Lomas Altas. His wife got an excellent job, and their child attended the local international school. There were horseback riding lessons, piano lessons, and golf lessons. They had a circle of friends in the expat community, and on weekends, could be found at a friend's home, or at a street-side café in Polanco, enjoying a meal and a glass of wine. He and his wife would go to museums on the weekends, take walks in the nearby park, holding hands like young lovers, and return home to a night of passion.

Life was good, indeed.

And then one day, it all ended. Francisco didn't come home from work. He had taken public transport that day to the office, and his mobile phone remained on his desk. He'd simply vanished, signing off on his last e-mails that day. There were no messages or Post-It notes, no phone calls or voicemails. His passport was on his nightstand at home. Francisco simply disappeared. Which was a problem, because he didn't exist, remember.

His wife, frightened and desperate, called his parent office in Florida and left a message. She also contacted the embassy's American Citizens' Services for consular assistance. She also called her family as well as Francisco's family back home. They had heard nothing. The embassy's checks with the local police authorities turned up nothing. Radio silence.

Finally, Francisco's wife called Father Ishmael, and let him know. He shared her deep concern and said he'd pray for her and Francisco, then meet her the next day for coffee in his office at the church.

The next day, Father Ishmael greeted her and hugged her. "Please come in my dear, let me offer you a coffee."

"Thank you, Padre. I am so scared. What will happen to Francisco? Where is he? What can I do?"

"We must be patient, and we must pray," Father Ishmael counseled. "The authorities will resolve this, I am sure. Let us pray the Rosary together."

What Francisco's wife couldn't know was that the Ambassador and CIA station chief had been informed, as had Sergio, back in Miami. They had quietly checked with all their local contacts, and the Ambassador and station had informed the Director of CISEN, Mexico's intelligence agency, as well as its counterpart to the FBI. NSA checks turned up nothing. The trail had gone cold.

CIA had reviewed every detail of Francisco's medical, psychological, and polygraph investigation, and had turned up nothing. Their psychologist back at headquarters had reviewed the file as well, and she saw no indication of suicide risk or suicidal behavior. Nor did Francisco's personality profile give any indication that he was type of man who would simply voluntarily disappear off the face of the earth. It didn't make sense.

But one hypothesis fit: Francisco had been kidnapped, most likely by a cartel, or by a hostile foreign intelligence service. But if the latter, analysis of e-mails and phone calls by NSA should have revealed *some* chatter (as it's known in espionage parlance). The international silence could only mean that a cartel had grabbed Francisco for their own purposes, and that time was critical. Every DEA agent, CIA officer, and embassy staffer in Mexico remembered the tragic case of DEA Special Agent Enrique Camarena, who had been kidnapped, tortured, and killed by a rival cartel while on assignment in Guadalajara, Mexico. And for those with short memories, every DEA office in Mexico had a portrait of Camarena on the wall, right next to those of the President, the Attorney General, and the director of the DEA.

The Ambassador call Father Ishmael that same day, asking, "Could you please come by today to give confession and to offer me the Sacrament of Reconciliation? Thank you, Father, and may God bless you. And may God bless Francisco, his wife and his child."

"Of course, Sir," said Father Ishmael. "I'll be over later today."

What else could he say?

The Ambassador

When Father Ishmael entered the Ambassador's office, their visit began differently from last time. The Ambassador welcomed him warmly and offered him not coffee, but a drink.

"Would you care for some scotch?"

"Sure, I'll take a scotch, neat, thank you very much."

And then he noticed another gentleman sitting quietly in the corner. He too had a scotch and was mouthing an unlit Cuban Montecristo.

The Ambassador turned and said politely, "Father Ishmael, please allow me to introduce you to one of our senior CIA officers, Ambrose."

Ambrose was tall, clean-shaven, and dressed in a three-piece brown suit. He wore Lucchese ostrich boots, an expensive tie, and his shirt and cufflinks were monogrammed.

A real dandy, Father Ishmael thought.

First, he was asked to sign a non-disclosure national security agreement, which he did. Then the CIA officer spoke. "I know this is a bit odd, but we've met before."

Now Father Ishmael recognized him. Of course...the man had occasionally attended the Mass for expats in his little parish. Ambrose had blue eyes, who could miss those? And his voice was smoky, soft, like a fine scotch. There was an odd mellow sense of calm about him, not the usual tension or ADHD-like hyperactivity seen in other CIA officers whom Father Ishmael had crossed paths with.

"My family and I have attended and enjoyed your Masses. I especially like your homilies about prudence and kindness. I try to teach that to my younger case officers. The keys to dealing with people in diplomacy, and for us, in recruiting agents, are kindness and empathy. Which brings me to my point. I know you, and we know you. I've been aware of your prior career, Padre. The good work you did—and now do—has not been lost upon us. And why I'm here today is because we, the Ambassador and I, and more importantly, our nation, need your help." He set aside his cigar and leaned forward. "What I'm about to tell you is known by very few people. It's known by me, the Ambassador, and by an American businessman stationed domestically. And now you. And I—no, we—need your gifts to help us. We need *your* prudence and kindness. Just like in your homily. Your nation needs you, Padre."

"I don't understand, sir. Why me? I am just an ordinary priest, serving a small parish in the middle of this great city. I take care of my flock, and I try to ease their sorrows and toils as they struggle to live in this huge, monstrous city, often far away from friends, family, and their home countries. What you seem to be talking about...." Ishmael shook his head. "I left the military years ago. I was no longer able to serve. I failed and struggled with my sins of omission and sins of commission. I have found peace ministering to my little flock, but that world I left behind? I'm sorry, gentlemen, but I must go. Thank you for your consideration."

A long silence followed. Finally, Ambrose stood and approached Father Ishmael, touching his arm softly. "Silence is a beautiful thing, is it not? You and I are alike. We both use silence in our work. Is silence not a weapon against evil, against the snares of the Devil? Is silence not a gift, during prayer, during sorrow, and in those quiet spaces of the confessional?" He shook his head. "Even though I have the ability and power, vested in the authority of the CIA's charter, to utilize our two greatest weapons, silence, and money, I lack your precious gifts. For you, Padre, silence is as much a part of you as the cross and cassock you wear. Perhaps I lack your faith, a faith tested many times, but put to a greater test, should you choose to accept this offer to assist us. Please, Padre...*por favor*, hear us out."

Ishmael leaned back in his chair, signaling his willingness to hear them out.

"The man whom you know as Francisco, a businessman and parishioner in your church, is indeed a businessman," Ambrose began. "But he's also another person, somebody else. He has many other names, many other identities, and numerous passports from different countries. He can be whatever he needs to be...whatever his nation needs him to be. He is responsible for some of the most sensitive and important intelligence operations and recruitments of the past decade. He is unique, like an artist. And espionage is his art. He is a master, and I'm in awe of him, as is his boss back in America, who recruited him to serve in this role, as a non-official CIA officer. So here you have it, Padre. Francisco has gone missing. We have combed all of our diplomatic and intelligence sources, as well as law enforcement sources, including at the highest levels of the Mexican government. We don't fully trust them, so we tapped into *all* of their communications using NSA resources, and all we found is silence. Nothing. It's not as if Francisco vanished, it's as though he never existed. We have not found any evidence suggesting a health issue or suicide. There is no evidence—yet—of homicide. There is no crime scene, no blood, no physical evidence."

Ishmael bowed his head and murmured a prayer for Francisco and his family. Then he looked up and met Ambrose's ice-blue gaze. "I'm hardly a crime-scene expert. I'm a priest. I still don't understand: Why me?"

"Padre, do you remember the motto of the elite military unit you served in? I do. It reads: *Send Me.* I know about your work in Latin America. You were awarded medals and honors. People were shocked when you retired after only a few years. So, I am calling you now, asking you to respond to that same call, *send me*. Let me explain. We have reason to believe that Francisco has been kidnapped, not by a hostile foreign intelligence service, but by one of the cartels. Not that the Russians or Chinese are not above such shenanigans. But they also know better—'do unto others,' etc. And there has been *zero* chatter from their channels about Francisco, or about any missing American, for that matter." Ambrose picked up his cigar and regarded it for a moment before setting it back down. "There is a gentleman who attends Mass at your church whom you know as Señor Lopez. He is a CEO of one of the largest banks in Mexico. But he is also the key go-between and liaison for the Mexican cartels, between the cartels—not cartel, but cartels, plural—and the Mexican government. He also liaises with other syndicates overseas such as the Mafia, the Russian mob, the Yakuza, and the Triads in China. He travels on a Mexican diplomatic passport. Now Lopez is no thug. He is an elegant gentleman, always impeccably dressed, unfailingly polite and generous. He is gracious to his clients, friends, and family. He's quite wealthy but is also a generous benefactor to charity and to the church. He is a close friend of several former (as well as the current) Mexican Presidents, as well as the last two directors of CISEN. So why you, Padre? We want you to be the go-between and carefully, patiently, and quietly, reach out to Señor Lopez. Tell him that you need his help regarding a fellow parishioner. His favorite restaurant is in Lomas Altas. But you may wish to approach him in church. Please be careful and use your best judgment. And do not delay, as time is of the essence. We have reason to believe that if the cartel doesn't kill Francisco, they will trade him to the Hezbollah or to Iran, as they are looking to expand their market reach in the Middle East." Ambrose approached Ishmael and touched his arm again. "We need you, Padre. Godspeed and many thanks. Please keep the Ambassador informed during your weekly Eucharistic Ministry."

Father Ishmael remained unsure, but when Ambrose's voice choked up, and he saw the faces of Francisco, his wife, and his child in his memory, Father Ishmael said, "I will help you." He touched his cross and the scapular which he wore daily around his neck, and quietly departed the embassy.

Señor Lopez

Señor Lopez went to Mass frequently, sometimes several times a week. He prayed the Rosary daily and found solace in its harmonies and repetitions, which eased the strain of his work, of his daily dealings with money, power, and corruption.

Today, as was typical, Lopez rose after Mass, needing to leave promptly for an appointment. So, it surprised him greatly when Father Ishmael approached him, greeting him personally.

"Buenos dias, Señor Lopez! *Que bueno*! How nice to see you. Do you have a moment? I need your advice."

This caught Señor Lopez even more off-guard, but he was not one to let his emotions show. So he smiled. "Of course, but regrettably not at this moment. Could you, say, meet me near my home tomorrow at 11 for coffee? I'll take you to the best coffee shop in Mexico. We can talk more freely there."

The next morning was beautiful, a light breeze making the city air as fresh as it could be. Father Ishmael hoped that this was a harbinger of good tidings. He loved spring—the colors, the birds, and the flowers in bloom throughout Mexico City's neighborhoods, especially the verdant, rich greenery of Lomas Altas. He took a taxi to the coffee shop and waited, arriving a few minutes early. He imagined that Señor Lopez did not like to be kept waiting. He was a banker, after all, with a life built upon on routines and punctuality.

Lopez arrived exactly at 11 a.m. in a black SUV with tinted windows. A door opened, and the driver opened his window and beckoned to Ishmael. "*Entre, por favor*, Padre."

He did so, joining Señor Lopez in the capacious back seat. The banker was sipping a bottle of Perrier and offered one to Father Ishmael. "*Buenos dias,* Padre. I thought that we could talk somewhere more private." He must have detected a glimmering of fear in Father Ishmael's eyes and quickly reassured him, "*Por favor, no tenga miedo, Padre.* We simply need to go somewhere where we can have more privacy."

Señor Lopez owned many homes in Mexico City, and they drove to Coyoacan, until they came to small, quaint studio apartment with an enchanting garden full of parakeets chirping away. "You'll like this apartment, Padre. We can sit in the garden and enjoy the best coffee in Mexico. The parakeets drown out other noises and distractions."

So they sat, at first quietly, absorbing the setting. As they drank coffee, Señor Lopez lit up a cigar, offering one to Father Ishmael, who declined. The coffee was indeed delicious. *Muy sabroso.*

"So, how can I be of help, Padre? *Como puedo ayudarle a usted?*"

Father Ishmael took a deep breath, smiled, and looked Señor Lopez in the eye. "I have a very delicate situation, Señor. One of my…one of *our*—we are all of the same flock, are we not?—parishioners has gone missing. I have checked with the relevant authorities, both on the Mexican side, as well as with American Consular Services. They have found no evidence of suicide, abandonment of his family, unexplained voluntary disappearance, or homicide. He has simply vanished. I want to do anything I can to help the family, so I'm turning to you, Señor Lopez. Here's a picture of his wife and their young child. As a father, husband, and now—*felicitaciones*—a grandfather, you can imagine their sorrow and grief."

Lopez took the photo politely and glanced at it, then set it on the table, face-down.

"The American consular authorities believe that Francisco has been kidnapped, most likely by one of the cartels. As his priest, I have offered to help, and that is why I am here today, requesting your assistance. Please help us find this young man, Señor Lopez. I know my sheep, and they know me. We are all of the same flock. We help each other. I hope you understand. In any case, I am in your debt and wish to express my deepest gratitude for any assistance you can provide."

Señor Lopez registered no change in facial expression or emotion but listened intently. He paused for a long time before responding, almost like a priest, or a well-trained psychotherapist. He rubbed his forehead gently and wiped his glasses. And then he spoke, so softly that Father Ishmael had to lean closer to hear each word. "Padre, I have no involvement with the cartels or with such persons, but as a banker, you are surely aware that I have many clients who come to me for financial and investment advice. I know many people in the business and political worlds. I live in a world of discretion and caution. I cannot imagine that the cartels would do such a horrible thing. While Mexico struggles with a raging kidnapping epidemic, kidnapping an American businessman is out of character and bad for business, unless some poor fool has gone rogue. I do not normally help gringos, who have often brought much harm to my country, which I love dearly. But I also love America. And you are not a gringo. You are also one of us, *un hombre de Mexico*. I know the story of your parents. Your Scots-Irish rancher father made your mother, a Mexicana, the love of his life. I know why you are here, and I know that you love this country. You have made it your own, you speak the language, and you appreciate our food, art, music, and most of all, our people, *nuestra communidad*. I know you, Padre. I know why you are here. You found your new home here, free at last, free at last, thank God almighty, I'm free at last. Ah, the timeless words of Dr. King. You've read Paz, right? Remember the last line of his greatest poem, <u>Sunstone</u>? The course of a river that turns, moves on, doubles back, and comes full circle, forever arriving. What genius, no? Paz was a true son of Mexico, but he too, was like you, Padre, a wandering soul. As you know, he served as a diplomat for many years, in France, India, and Japan." Lopez paused again and sighed deeply. "You are my friend, and you are a son of Mexico as well as America. Because of this, I will make some inquiries and try to be of help. But no promises, Padre. And I'd suggest no media or publicity. It is such an American thing, to get the national news involved in a personal tragedy. But if you are correct, and if your friend has been kidnapped, then publicity will get him killed…and now, because of your involvement, possibly you as well. Let's meet again next week at the same place. *Vaya con Dios, Padre.*"

CISEN

After several days had passed, Father Ishmael felt uncertain, even a bit unmoored. He no longer knew to expect. He thought, I must pray about this, and trust in Him. He found himself back in the embassy, where he waited to brief the Ambassador, while giving him the Eucharistic Sacrament during their weekly time. He had called a cab to take him back to his apartment, when a black SUV with official government plates pulled up and several operatives got out.

"*Entre en nuestro vehiculo, por favor, Padre.*"

He did so. "*A donde vamos?* Where are we going?"

"Patience, Padre," said the driver. "*Tiene que tener paciencia, verdad?*"

They drove for several miles to a nondescript house, actually a small apartment in San Angel. But this was no ordinary apartment. It was a government safe house, used by CISEN, Mexico's intelligence agency, an organization analogous to the CIA and FBI. When he walked into the apartment, he was greeted by an elderly, courtly gentleman, the Director of CISEN. Ishmael knew that the old spymaster had studied as a younger man at Harvard and Stanford, so it was no surprise that he spoke perfect, accent-free English.

"I apologize for grabbing you off the street so suddenly, Padre, but sometimes we have to do things quietly and with care. Let me begin by thanking you for coming to meet with me. It means a lot. As you may or may not know, your Ambassador met with our President to discuss the matter at hand. We know about your meeting with the Ambassador and his senior CIA officer. Ambrose is an old friend, *un buen amigo por siempre.* We go way back. And the Ambassador and I are old friends as well. Mexico is grateful for his diplomacy, grace, and goodwill. Oh, and by the way, I know about your little coffee klatsch, *poco han charlado, con* Señor Lopez. *El es tambien un buen amigo,* a classy person, *una persona buen educada.* He and I play golf together every week. Perhaps you could join us one day…. *Quizas, quizas, quizas.* So let me offer some gentle advice, Padre. I don't mean to be presumptuous, for you are a true hombre and man of the cloth."

"I realize that you, the Ambassador, and Ambrose are concerned that your 'businessman' colleague has been kidnapped by one of the cartels. Please don't look surprised. We do our homework. We have kept a close eye on Francisco ever since he arrived. We have tracked his travels. Why would an American businessman go to Havana or Caracas on an EU passport?" He raised a hand preeemptively. "*Por favor, Padre.* Don't say anything, do not offend my sensibility. This is our country. I realize that as a priest, you wish to help one of the members of your flock. That is proper and just. But please be careful. You see, I worry that if *we* know what you're up to, then so do the cartels. I understand: you possess great discretion, and both the Ambassador and Ambrose are trusting you and relying upon your judgment. I too admire this elan and way of doing things, and would do so, and have done likewise in many different places. But *please* be careful. *Cuidese, Padre.* For the cartels won't invite you for coffee and a chat, as I have done. The tend to be very rough. And if or when that happens, neither I, nor the Ambassador, nor my friend Ambrose, will be able to help you. Thank you again, I appreciate your listening and being here today."

And with that, the bodyguards reappeared and drove Father Ishmael back to his apartment.

Prayers

Father Ishmael was at a loss, even dumbfounded. He was struck by CISEN's reach and knowledge of the situation and his involvement. He thought that he had left that old life behind. Recent events had reopened old wounds, and rekindled a forgotten part of his past, and his psyche. There were fears, emotions, losses, and pain. This in turn, brought confusion. Whenever he felt lost or confused, he found it helpful to pray the Rosary, both in Spanish and English. This calmed his mind, his worries, and his senses. While he was praying, there was a knock on his door. It was late at night, and he hadn't ordered any deliveries. He opened the door and saw no one. He looked down on the step and saw an envelope. The envelope contained a recent family photo of Francisco, his wife, and their child.

He became worried and wondered what to do next. It was tempting to reach out to the Ambassador for his weekly Eucharistic Sacrament, but it was early in the week, and it wasn't due for several days. He remembered the words from Proverbs, counseling prudence. But he also remembered his earlier, vestigial, military intelligence training, where his work in the unit taught him to wait, to avoid rushing into things, to be still, and to remain unhurried. *Be the water, my friend.*

Mass that week was odd. Ambrose was there, as was Señor Lopez. So was Francisco's wife and their child. They were dressed elegantly, and she smiled as she passed him for Holy Communion. She was desperately trying to be strong for her child and put on her bravest face. But she clearly held it together in only the most vulnerable and fragile way. Father Ishmael had counseled many kidnap victims and families, and he knew their pains and sorrows. They lived in a suspended world of grief and fear, of not knowing whether or when their loved one would return. Some cracked under the strain, went mad with grief.

He smiled at her and moved to the next parishioner.

Señor Lopez did likewise, accepting communion with a smile, then leaving through the chapel entrance.

Ambrose winked before departing, clearly anticipating his first cigar of the day.

DEA

His next visit to the Ambassador brought another surprise. This time, not only were Ambrose and the Ambassador present, but another gentleman waited with them in the opulent office.

The Ambassador offered them each a drink. "Scotch, gentlemen?"

"Of course, thank you, Mr. Ambassador."

"Good morning, Padre. Care for a drink?"

"It's a bit early for me, thanks, just coffee."

The third man introduced himself as Johnny. He was the DEA chief. He wore nicely pressed slacks, a bolo tie of Hopi design, and black Lucchese ostrich boots. He had a goatee and Fu Manchu mustache. He had various tattoos on his neck and hands. Clothing aside, he looked like a biker. In truth, he had worked undercover for years, infiltrating biker gangs dealing in drugs and guns. Like the others in attendance, he spoke fluent Spanish. He began the conversation.

"It's nice to meet you, Padre. We're thankful for your time. Ambrose and the Ambassador have briefed me about your meetings with Señor Lopez and the Director of CISEN, but I already knew. That's how my folks and I stay alive here. We all remember Kiki Camarena. I knew him personally and he was a friend, I knew his wife and kids. I was godfather to his children. So you definitely understand where I'm coming from. The cartels play for keeps, and they don't play nice. Anyways, I was chatting over lunch this week with a high-level source, and they know all about your little *sitas* with Lopez and CISEN. Padre, by nature you're a keeper of secrets. The seal of the confessional, right? The Sacrament of Reconciliation, *verdad*? As a lapsed Catholic"—he smiled sheepishly—"I get that. But there are no secrets in Mexico. At any rate, my source tells me that the cartels know nothing, *nada*, about Francisco. But Lopez has another proposition.... He wants to meet with you next week, same time, same place. Now, I visited him too but he wouldn't say what it's about, except that *you'd* be able to enlighten us more. Only thing he'd say was something about *la niña*. Be cautious around Lopez, okay? He is not what he appears to be. *Vaya con Dios, Padre.*"

The Girl

Father Ishmael met Señor Lopez at the same café, same time. A car was waiting and took him to a different, more private garden at another banker's home somewhere in Lomas Altas.

Señor Lopez was gracious as always and offered an espresso and some cookies. He lit a Montecristo, blew a series of expanding smoke rings, then spoke softly: "I must ask you something. One of my sources in the government who's close to the cartels said that they want to make a trade. But it's not what you're thinking. They don't have Francisco. They think that he's likely dead, as there are no traces of him anywhere or at any time since his disappearance. There is, as you'd say in the vernacular, no proof of life. I am so very sorry for the loss of your friend, Padre. But I'd like to know… do you know this girl? Here is a picture of her and her mother. See, the cartels know about your prior military background, and they've followed your career with great interest."

Father Ishmael was dumbfounded. He did not recognize the girl, who was approximately eight years of age. But he immediately recognized Marisa, the girl's pretty mother—her face, her dark curls, and her figure. How could he not? They had been together on so many nights…holding hands as they walked in Chapultepec Park, hiking up the pyramids. How could he forget such love? Other

36

memories flooded him: of making love for hours on a lazy after-noon, siestas spent together with no worries and no cares.

He had read Neruda's love poems to her, and she back to him. *Cuerpo de mujer, blancas colinas, muslos blancos, te pareces al mundo tu actitud de entrega.* They would laugh, weep, and return to a night of love, only sleeping after their bodies were finally spent. She had dark eyes, flashing with passion, and they'd twinkle when she was happy. But now, recalling how he had departed, without even a goodbye kiss, broke his heart. A tear streaked down his face. He looked away from Señor Lopez, but the older man, ever observant, surely saw him wipe his eye.

Señor Lopez let the silence between them settle in, for he knew its power and value. "The mother and her daughter—your daughter—are right here in Mexico City. My contacts in the government have proposed a trade. They will let her and the girl, *tu niña*, go and begin a new life in America. El Norte. Imagine that…. *Can* you imagine, Padre? A new life, a new beginning. What they want is the release from prison of a leading cartel leader's daughter. She is innocent. She was arrested because of a wiretap, and because she, against her husband's better judgment, agreed to translate and interpret a deal, on one given day—just one day!—when their usual interpreter was sick. She, like your former beloved, has not seen her husband or children for years. She has not known their joys, sorrows, smiles, kisses, *abrazos*, or the tenderness of her husband's embrace. Padre, you are not a true gringo. You too have Mexican blood, and you understand Paz's great work *El Laberinto de Soledad*. In Mexico, the most important thing is family. It is everything. I need your help, Padre. And for that, I will help you, your former love, and your daughter. They have green cards in hand, and passports, tickets, and a place to stay with relatives in LA. Your daughter is excited about Disneyland and baseball. She wants to go to a Dodgers game. Imagine that Padre, *por Dios mio! Baseball.* So American. And we too love baseball, because baseball is not only about sport and

America, but it's about family. Take me out to the ballgame…isn't that right? Will you help me, Padre?"

Father Ishmael thought for a long time. Could Señor Lopez feel his shame, his loss? He had never known about the child. But one look at the picture told him that Señor Lopez was not lying. She was his daughter. She had his eyes and his facial features, his countenance. He had no choice.

"Yes, count me in."

"*Muchas gracias, Padre.* I will be in touch next week about the arrangements. Please be careful, for if there is any deception on the part of your government or the Mexican authorities, the deal is off, and I will not be able to vouch for the mother's and girl's safety. You do understand, *no?*"

The Deal

Señor Lopez handled all the details like those of a complex business transaction. The exchange would take place at El Angel, just a few blocks from the American Embassy. Señor Lopez and Father Ishmael would be at the exchange. The President, Director of CISEN, and Director of the Mexican state police were aware, as were the Ambassador, Ambrose, and Johnny. The time was set for 1159 in the morning. It would start with a coded phone call to Señor Lopez.

It was a beautiful day in Mexico City. It had rained the week before, and the breezes blew away the pollution, leaving clear blue skies. Father Ishmael was nervous that morning, and he prayed the Rosary. He also went to confession, asking for forgiveness for his many sins, for his abandonment of his daughter and her mother. He didn't know why, but he knew that was a lie. On their last night together, they had made love with greater feeling and intensity than before. She had wept, and had told him, "*Por favor, no me dejes, mi amor.* Don't ever leave me." And now he would see her again, and the daughter he had never met, for the first time. Even after his confession and praying of the Rosary, he felt a deep sense of guilt and shame. But penance would come later. For now, he had worn his nicest suit to the exchange. He wanted to show them his best. Today, he was not a Franciscan or a Jesuit. He wasn't a priest, but a father, a lover, a man, *un hombre.*

39

Johnny would be at the exchange too, watching from a nearby safe house and observation post. Ambrose and his assets would work undercover at the scene, never seen or heard. There were snipers, CIA paramilitaries. But the key assets were called The Watchers. They were contractors, who could blend in. There was the *abuela* with her cart of fruits. The taco vendor. And the skateboarder, who did tricks while skating in the middle of traffic every day at El Angel. There was the drug addict, smoking pot and looking for a needle that he had dropped. And the young lovers, walking, kissing, holding hands. They too were Mexico, part of its pulse, its life, *toda la vida*. *Gracias a la Vida*, sang Chavela Vargas.

He saw the government SUV first. Señor Lopez got out and walked toward the exchange point. After him, stepping out of the government vehicle, dressed in a classic dress, looking resplendent and then holding Señor Lopez' arm, was the daughter of the cartel leader. The *jefe* himself was not in attendance, but his emissaries were. So, surely, were *his* watchers. Oddly, Ishmael saw no cartel security personnel.

What the government could not know, what Ambrose and Johnny could not know, what even Señor Lopez could not know, was the that the cartel leader—El Viejo—had hedged his bets. The entire circle at El Angel was ringed with C4 plastic explosives, triggered to go off with a coded phone call if the exchange were betrayed.

Another SUV approached, letting out Marisa and their daughter. They too were dressed in their Sunday best, both wearing colorful skirts. They walked slowly toward the exchange, toward Señor Lopez and the cartel leader's wife. They passed, and the wife got into the vehicle, and it was done. Simple as that. Marisa and her daughter kept walking toward him and Señor Lopez, who was effusive, smiling, and gracious, extending his arms to them.

Suddenly, Father Ishmael felt an odd sensation, as if something were wrong. The girl and her mother showed no joy, no emotion, no fear, and no tears. They shook Señor Lopez's hand formally. Marisa looked at him, and then he knew. *Puta Madre! Damn you,*

40

Lopez. He wanted to kill him. But it was too late. Señor Lopez, the girl, and her mother were in the SUV, and had quickly departed, leaving Ishmael standing alone, in the middle of Mexico City, next to El Angel, as traffic roared about him on the roundabout. There was no Marisa nor their daughter. And the cartel leader's daughter was free, and had vanished.

My God, My God, why have You forsaken me? He sat down and wept. All he could remember afterward were Johnny and Ambrose cradling him in their arms, saying, "Come on, Padre, it's okay now, you're safe, it's over."

CIA Headquarters

There would be no funeral service for Francisco. But there was something else. At the Wall of Honor, a stonemason chiseled, polished, and carved another nameless star on the Wall. The Director was there, as were Ambrose, the Ambassador, and Sergio. Francisco's wife and child also attended. They stood for a picture with the Director, and he gave them an American flag. He thanked them for their service, and for giving Francisco to the nation, and for allowing him to serve.

Father Ishmael was there too. He shook hands with the Ambassador and Ambrose, and embraced Francisco's wife and child. He prayed with them, off in a quiet corner of the ceremonial hall. He could only say, "I am so deeply sorry for your loss." And then he was gone.

It was over, another chapter would begin. The Ambassador had competed his term and would no return to the private sector. He kissed Francisco's wife and hugged her child and wished them peace, solace. Ambrose shook hands and left before they could see his tears. He too had left Mexico and would soon be posted to Bogota. There were other challenges, other places, other lands, and most of all, other men and women who served. Ambrose worshiped the CIA and he admired its people, their service and dedication to country. But he had too many friends who had become stars on the Wall. He wondered how much more he could take.

And so they departed, leaving Francisco's star, the Book of Remembrance, and an American flag. It was a sacred place, and the stars were always lit at night. Stars of wonder, stars of courage, stars of failure, and most of all, stars of loss.

El Viejo

One day Father Ishmael was leaving his parish and walking to his car, when a black SUV with no license plates pulled up. A clutch of bodyguards, all dressed in suits and wearing sunglasses with pistols drawn, ordered him into the vehicle: "*Entre, por favor, Padre. Mas rapido, por favor. Silencio, por favor. No grite, por fa.*" A black hood was placed over his head, and his hands were tied with plastic zip ties. He struggled to breathe and wondered who his kidnappers were. CISEN? The cartel? The federales? Nobody spoke. The car took a circuitous route through downtown. Father Ishmael didn't know it, but another passenger got into the vehicle near the huge outdoor market, Tepito. The passenger spoke to the driver, but his Spanish sounded elegant and soft. The bodyguards remained silent. Oddly, the passenger smelled of fresh cologne… something nice. And expensive.

After an hour or so, the vehicle arrived at its destination, a large, two-story villa, ringed with tall hedges, in Lomas Altas. His hood was removed, and a maid appeared, offering water, fruits, and coffee. Across from him sat his fellow passenger, wearing a linen suit with a yellow tie. Father Ishmael smelled the cologne again; he had an acute sense for it after all those years of hearing confessions in tiny booths. The gentleman looked elderly, maybe in his late 60s, and distinguished. He was Mexican but spoke accent-free English.

"*Buenos dias, Padre.* I apologize, *lo siento,* for the impolite manner in which you were brought here, but I'd nevertheless like to welcome you to my home. Oh, you're probably wondering, who am I? You need not know my name, but I am called El Viejo. I am a businessman with many interests in various sectors. I wish to thank you for your role in getting my daughter released from prison safely. I recognize that such things are not easy in this country. And of course your ex-girlfriend Marisa and your daughter are safely located in LA. They have a lovely apartment in Brentwood, right near UCLA. Would you like her address and cell phone, Padre? My family and I find Brentwood to be nice, as we frequently go to UCLA for specialized medical care."

"Why am I here, Señor? Why did you bring me here? Are you not endangering me?"

"On the contrary, Padre, the authorities know of your work, as do we. And of course, as do the Nuncio, Ambassador, CIA station chief, and the DEA attaché. I want to not only thank you, Padre, but to let you know that I may at times request your help in a sensitive kidnap matter. Normally, I prefer that such things be handled more directly, if you understand my meaning. But there are other times when a gentler approach is best. And that's where I need you. You will help, no? Also, I am sorry for the loss of your friend. We of course knew all about Francisco and had observed his many talents in business. I wish that I had more guys like him in my organization! *Que bueno,* right?"

Father Ishmael thanked the elderly gentleman, having no choice but to say, "Of course, my services are at your disposal. Thank you for your directness and honesty. Helping others is my duty, my cross to bear. I serve others so that I may better serve Him."

El Viejo smiled. For the head of Mexico's largest cartel, he had a gentle face and kind, soft eyes. He said, "You're very gracious, and you are free to go, Padre. Here is my cell phone number. Please call me if I can ever be of help to you. Thank you for your generosity. *Vaya con Dios.*"

A bodyguard placed a hood over his head, and he was taken to the vehicle. No zip-ties this time, thankfully.

When he emerged an hour later at his parish, he couldn't stop shaking. But he was alive.

The Nuncio

Father Ishmael continued to minister to his flock in Mexico City. He never saw Señor Lopez again, for he too had vanished. He was no longer in the news, in the society pages, or in business trade publications. It was as if Lopez, like Francisco, had ceased to exist. Or as if he had never existed. But there was a flock to attend to. There were Masses, homilies, baptisms, First Communions, marriages, the Anointing of the Sick, and visits to hospitals, homes, hospices, and other places for last rites. But there was more.

After the release of the cartel leader's daughter, Father Ishmael's reputation for discretion and negotiation had grown. Almost every wealthy Mexican family—and even many expats—knew somebody who had been kidnapped. Without wanting to—for he hated the fear, the loathing, and the physical sickness that each kidnapping caused him—he became a go-between and negotiator in a number of such cases. He was discreet, diligent, and could be trusted. Embassies called upon him for his skills. Over the past few years, he had worked—successfully—on nearly a dozen kidnapping cases. Some of those were sensitive cases involving diplomats, their spouses or children, Catholic priests, the cartels, or businessman at the highest level. Father Ishmael felt lucky, for he had never lost a hostage. Or was it not luck, but rather, God's grace, His grace, and His blessings?

Little surprised Father Ishmael. But one day he was indeed caught off-guard when, after Mass, a diplomatic vehicle was waiting, and the driver asked, "*Entre, por favor.*"

Ishmael did not recognize the plates until the vehicle pulled up to the residence of the Papal Nuncio, who had been posted to Mexico City for many years. He had never met the Nuncio, who hailed from Colombia. He had been an archbishop in Bogota, and had developed contacts with the government, the cartels, and the FARC. He was an odd person: short and chubby, even a bit fat. He waddled slowly, and spoke languidly, choosing each word precisely. He had bushy eyebrows and smiled easily. He giggled and laughed at jokes, including his own. It was rather disarming, causing many to miss his intelligence, listening abilities, empathy, patience, and prudence. He had that sense of making any parishioner or interlocutor feel as if they were the only person—and certainly the most important—in the room. He had piercing eyes that he'd close while thinking, humming softly to himself, like an orchestra conductor. He might switch to giggling or even ribald laughter, and would often say, "Oh, that's SO funny." But this too was a deception. He knew everybody, and not only in the diplomatic corps. He played golf with the President, and dined with business leaders, politicians, and cultural figures. He had lunched frequently with the late Señor Lopez. He was a favorite of the Pope and had organized his Holiness's last visit to Mexico.

The Nuncio greeted Father Ishmael with a huge smile and an *abrazo.* "Welcome, Padre! I have heard so much about you, and I'm delighted that you could join me. For we have much to discuss. May I offer you some coffee or tea? I also have biscuits. Come now, Padre, they're quite tasty. *Muy sabrosos.*"

Ishmael accepted graciously while waiting for the rotund diplomat to get to the point.

"I've followed your career closely, and the Vatican is aware of it as well. Not bad for a Jesuit, no? Ha! *Que buena onda!* Well, the church has need of your extraordinary skills. In fact, the Secretary of State chatted with me last week, and he agreed with my proposal. If you accept, you'd fly to Rome for additional training before your next posting. So, please listen carefully. God calls in His strange ways, don't you agree? Time, talent, and treasure. We all have gifts, given to us by God, and we're obligated to use them to the fullest. This is true of you, and it's equally true of me."

Ishmael nodded agreeably but already he felt the incipient pain of leaving his parishioners, his parish, his adopted city.

"Your work in delicate negotiations involving diplomacy and kidnappings has not gone unnoticed. You have a knack for it, a gift of sorts. I know about your work with the Americans regarding Francisco. I see the hurt in your eyes, and I'm sorry for the loss of your parishioner, your friend. It is God's will, *verdad*? *Palabra de Dios*. And I know about your work involving many other *secuestrados*, and your ability to return them home safely to their loved ones. I understand this rather personally, Padre, because I lived in Bogota for many years. I understand the horror of such things, and like you, counseled and prayed for many victims. You know how such things often end. But it is God's will."

The smaller man shrugged, as if in solidarity. Then his gaze focused sharply on Ishmael.

"And it is now God's will that you leave Mexico. It is time. I know that it's difficult to leave your flock and this country, which you have grown to love. But the Church needs your services elsewhere."

Father Ishmael continued to hide his emotions, but he was stunned and chose to remain silent, not trusting himself with a verbal reaction in the moment. He blinked, and without conscious thought, reacted openly: "Why, your excellence? Why me, why now? Have I done something wrong? Have I offended the Church? Is my faith and work not enough? What more do you ask of me? I have nothing more to give. I belong here."

The Nuncio listened carefully. He bit his lip and tugged at his collar. He rubbed his forehead and poured some more coffee. "Padre, it's not my decision. The Secretary of State of the Holy See

49

has made this request, and even his Holiness the Holy Father is aware of my proposal. Allow me to explain. We will be sending you to Russia, to Moscow, where you will minister to a community of Spanish-speaking expats. They need you there, Padre. Moscow is a beautiful city with a rich history. It is the seat of power and represents the greatness of Russia. But it's not an easy place. Our priests are often harassed by the local secret services, the FSB. They don't play nicely. They will stop you, check your papers, tap your phone and e-mail, and harass you. They may even detain you for a day or so, just to frighten you. They will follow you on the Metro and infiltrate your Masses. So it will not be easy, not at all. We have a priest, a missionary in Tver, who has gone missing. The FSB is holding him incommunicado. He has not been allowed consular access or access to the Nuncio there. He is a dual-national American and Mexican citizen. We would like for you to find him and quietly negotiate his release with the Russian government. Please, Padre. You will be given funds to start a small parish in Moscow. You may call it Our Lady of Sorrows, *Nuestra Madre de la Tristeza*. You will not be accredited to the Nuncio, but we will make you an apostolic delegate without portfolio. You will be issued a diplomatic passport, but you are never to use it when traveling in Russia. The Americans don't know about the details, but our Nuncio there has made the American Ambassador—who is a faithful member of our church—aware of your arrival. You leave for Rome next month for some additional training and meetings at the diplomatic academy. Please start studying Russian too. You will need it. It helps break the ice with the Russians. Oh, and *vaya con Dios, Padre*."

Moscow

Father Ishmael arrived in Moscow several months later. He arrived at Sheremetyevo Airport, still a dingy remnant of the '80s. It had a peculiar odor, and the walls were stained, aging, and moldy in places. But driving from the airport to downtown, and later seeing the sights, amazed and awed him. He welcomed the grandeur and spent a week taking in the city's most magnificent offerings: the Kremlin, St. Basil's Cathedral, the Bolshoi, the Tretyakov Gallery, Novodevichy Cemetery, and Lenin's Tomb in Red Square.

His Russian hosts were gracious, and plied him with wine, women, and song; there were trips to the dacha, where one could take a sauna bath (a *banya*), drink a liter of vodka, and have a large peasant woman with meaty hands give a vigorous massage before smacking one's backside with birch switches, 'to make your nerves feel open and pure.' In the winter, this would be followed by several minutes of sprinting naked in the snow, being doused with ice water—it possessed healing properties—and dried off before returning to the sauna. And there would be feasts! Lamb shashlik, soup, cabbage, wild boar meat, sturgeon, caviar, and blini, all washed down with Georgian wines and vodka. Staying initially at the old—now torn-down—Hotel Moskva near Red Square, he would be greeted by a fierce *dezhurnaya*—the ladies who ran the place, kept order, and reported all activity to the local branch of the FSB.

Father Ishmael enjoyed walking in Moscow. Every weekend, he would take a long walk down to the Moscow River, along the bank, known as the *berezhnaya*. He appreciated its wide sidewalks, its serenity. And then there was The Arbat, with its quaint shops, cafés, historic 19th-century architecture, and of course, famed street artists. One drew a portrait of him in 5 minutes for the equivalent of $200.

"$200 for 5 minutes?"

"No, my friend, $200 for 20 years—and 5 minutes."

Walking, he could hear the voice of the late Bulat Okudzhava, the great poet and bard, singing that haunting song, 'Arbat's Romance.' And then there was Patriarch's Pond.... Sitting on a bench, he half-expected the Devil of Bulgakov's masterpiece *The Master and Margarita* to sit next to him on a bench: "One should never talk to strangers."

And so it went. Long walks, silences, a coffee here and there, and he slowly embraced Moscow, its stolid splendor and delights. There were blini, cappuccinos, and herring, downed with a shot of vodka. He observed, sitting in a café, Moscow's entirety, and its humanity. There was the oligarch and his family, dressed to the nines, with their bodyguards nearby, always watching, observing. They never wore sunglasses, but had on dark suits, with guns in shoulder holsters. Once, as he was exiting a café, he got too close to the oligarch. A bodyguard gently steered him away, patting him down as he did so. His fingertips were gentle and soft, like his voice, "This way, please. Thank you." Like an artist playing Chopin.

There were others. The pretty Russian girl, sitting with her boyfriend, holding hands as lovers do, her eyes sparkling, and the boy not even noticing the froth of her cappuccino on her lips. Father Ishmael crossed himself for having a sinful thought. *Before the action comes the thought.* And in the corner, an old lady, a babushka, with her old, ratty purse, staring at the waiters and the young lovers. She looked like an old crone, exactly like the one whom Raskolnikov murdered in the opening of *Crime and Punishment*. How dare they hold hands in public! No manners. This too, was Moscow.

For a native Texan used to scorching hot summers, Father Ishmael dreaded the cold, long Russian winters. He learned about icicles, and he learned to love snow. He reveled in the snows of Gorky Park, the woods along the highways leading to Domodedovo airport, lined with white birch trees for miles and miles. Nothing but white, shimmering, and majestic snow. The Russians loved the snow and the cold. It was part of Russia, who they were. He bought a Russian fur hat, made of sable, a *shapka*. During these months, he saw another Russia, one more alive and real. Russia was snow, ice, and cold. As only it could be. The snows and cold that defeated Napoleon and Hitler. That too, was Russia.

The chapel was small but managed to hold approximately 100 people. Most were expats from the Hispanic community, a handful of diplomats, businesspersons, and students. Masses were in Spanish. There were even a few Mexican-American parishioners as well. He noticed a tall gentleman, wearing a brown suit, cowboy boots, and a brightly colored shirt. His wife, originally from Mexico, was there with their child. It was only later, as they left, that he found himself weeping softly, not knowing why.

"*Dios, por mio*, why did You take Francisco from us?" He wondered about Francisco's wife and child. How were they faring? Where was the justice, the mercy? He spoke of justice and mercy in his weekly homilies. It was easy to speak of such things. *La bondad, la justicia*. He taught them not to sorrow, for Moscow did not believe in tears. He spoke of hope, of how Jesus was always with us, even in the darkest, coldest nights of Russia's long winters. He spoke to them of spring, of the anticipation of Easter. Surely, yes, Christ is Risen. He is risen for us and to wash away our sins. *Khristos voskres*. He taught his flock that one can find Jesus anywhere, even in Moscow. In the old lady, stooped over, begging for coins in the street tunnels, *perekhods*, with their smell of filth, urine, and grime. In the police officers, the GAI, standing around, smoking, harassing foreigners for a bribe with their white batons, their *palki*. The ticket-collector at the subway, clearly a character from one of Gogol's novels.

Surveillance and harassment were omnipresent. His apartment was bugged for video and audio, as were his phones, both landline and cellphone. He would hear crackling sounds, pops, whistles, and beeps while talking on the phone. Or he'd return to his apartment and notice that somebody had been there. Once, they left the coffee pot on. He smelled the aroma as he walked in the door. This too was Russia. Because of his past, he understood and accepted such things. But his flock suffered, and he frequently had to console them. A weeping spouse, who had been pulled over by the FSB in front of her kids, the police constantly demanding, "*Dokument, dokument, dokument.*" The young office worker, speaking of being stripped, violated.

This too, was Russia.

The Nuncio, Moscow

One day there was a new parishioner at Mass. He was young, neatly attired, in a priestly collar and wearing a dark suit. He spoke English fluently with an American accent and approached Father Ishmael after Mass.

"The Nuncio would like to see you now, Padre. Please come with me and join him for tea or coffee. You're probably wondering who I am. I am a secretary for the Nuncio. I answer phones, check his correspondence, things like that."

This struck Father Ishmael as odd. The young man spoke perfect Spanish, English and Russian. *Hmm.* They rode the Metro together, only a few stops to the Nunciature.

The Nuncio dismissed his secretary and welcomed Father Ishmael. His voice and handshake were firm, and he had meaty hands. He had on a class ring, and looked like football player, which he had been. "Oh, yeah, I played linebacker for Holy Cross before my life changed and I heard God's call and entered the priesthood. They found out that I am very good at languages—I speak fluent Slovene and Russian—so here I am. Yeah, Father, it's a long way from Cleveland."

He looked around his office, as if missing something. "Have some tea, please, oh and the Russian tea cakes are heavenly, if I may."

"Thank you, your excellency, it's my pleasure to meet you. But please explain, why am I here?"

"What a wonderful question, Father Ishmael! Why are we here? What is our purpose? We are here to serve God, right? And so, I am asking you to serve, and to help us out."

"But I already serve my parish, your excellency. What more do you ask?"

"We don't ask more, Father. We only ask enough. God does not give us more than we can handle. So please hear me out."

Ishmael inclined his head in hesitant agreement.

"A local missionary priest—he ministers to his tiny flock in Tver—has gone missing. He has been in Russia for several years, and is originally from Mexico, although he is an American citizen, and therefore dual national. Because he learned fluent Russian, the FSB doesn't believe that he's a priest. They are convinced that he's an American spy, working under deep cover for CIA, what they call an Illegal. I spoke with the American Ambassador at a recent reception, and he assured me that this priest has no US government connections. The US government does not use priests as under-cover agents, or what they call NOCs, for non-official cover. Of course, the SVR and FSB do this often, so they assume likewise with the Americans. At any rate, he has not been allowed any consular access. We have no idea where he is, or whether he's even alive. We'd like for you to make some inquiries and to quietly assist both the Nunciature and the American Embassy. It's all a bit odd and delicate. The Americans can't be involved beyond a consular level, and the Vatican can't do much, as he has no diplomatic status in Russia. He's just a priest, after all."

Ishmael cleared his throat. "I see. But you realize, I'm a new-comer here myself. My connections are—"

"Not to worry," the nuncio interrupted. "I have been briefed about your work in this area, Father Ishmael. I know of your diplomatic, negotiation, and pastoral skills. You have a gift, and we need your time, treasure, and talent. The Ambassador told me that—he and his

Country Team suspect this—the FSB not only has the priest, but that they're willing to trade him for one of their people, an arms dealer in an American federal prison. The Americans want you to quietly help broker a deal. They have reached out to the FSB, and they didn't get a yes, but they didn't get a *nyet* either. The FSB liaison said, Let us think about it. You have a meeting tomorrow with the Ambassador, and he'd like for you to hear his confession, and grant him Holy Communion. He is expecting you at 9, sharp. Please be there. Good luck, Father Ishmael. Or they say in Mexico, *vaya con Dios.*"

The Ambassador, Moscow

Father Ishmael didn't know what to expect. The Ambassador's official biography spoke of his expertise, built over long years of service in Russia and the former USSR. He was from the heartland, and had grown up speaking Russian, for his mother was a White Russian émigré.

Quoting Corinthians 13, he told Ishmael, "When I was a child, I talked like a child, I thought like a child, reasoned like a child. When I became a man, I put the ways of childhood behind me. Russia made me a man, Father. Thank you for coming, please have some coffee."

He poured and served. Not like a typical Ambassador. Being from middle America, he had the smile, friendliness, and ease of a corn farmer from Nebraska. He had a kind manner about him, a way of making people comfortable. He spoke Russian beautifully, which he said amazed the Russians. He would sing songs, he knew the songs of Bulat Okudzhava, Vladimir Vissotsky, and Ivan Talkov by heart. He recited Pushkin, Brodsky, Akhmatova, and Mandelstam, pages and pages of it.

As a young diplomat and consular officer at large, he had traveled throughout the former Soviet Union and studied Russian—immersion-style—for a year in Tver. He savored swimming and fishing in the Volga, and his first love had been a Russian girl, whom he had romanced during his time there. The Ambassador liked people, and his body language had slowly evolved, to where he looked and acted like a Russian. He found himself chatting with Russians from all walks of life: the Metro ticket seller, the old man in the café, the gypsy cab driver, the street seller, and yes, even the FSB officer assigned to follow him. But this was a ruse. What the Russians didn't know is that he had earlier in his career, been trained as a CIA case officer, prepared in grueling training—lasting several years—for a Moscow assignment. The hardest training had been surveillance. For the final exam, the agency had taken him to New York, after a week of sleep deprivation, with no car or money and the FBI on his tail, and had told him, "See you at headquarters in a week. Don't fuck it up, Corn Pone." He somehow passed this test. He only traveled at night and slept in fields in New Jersey. Even slept for two days in a garbage truck, knowing the FBI wouldn't look for him there. He then hopped a train like a 'trainspotter' and showed up in Baltimore, wandering among its homeless population, only to appear at headquarters a few days later, showered, shaved, well-fed, while wearing a nice new suit. Ultimately, his assignment had fallen through when a Russian spy re-defected and blew his cover. So off he went, following a more conventional diplomatic path. And here he was, chatting with Father Ishmael over coffee after receiving Holy Communion.

"We need your help, Father. I have spoken to the Nuncio, and he has given his blessing. I, on behalf of the American Embassy and the US government, appreciate your help in this very delicate matter. As you know, an American dual-national priest living in Tver has likely been arrested by the FSB and been charged with espionage. He is being held in Lefortovo, a rather nasty place. The Russians are not granting consular access, and we've filed diplomatic notes and formal complaints with the Foreign Ministry. I have good contacts here after serving here for many years. But, Father, they'd won't touch this. Either they change the subject or hang up when I make an inquiry. There may be some hope, however. Our CIA station chief has regular meetings with his FSB contact. They drink vodka together, eat blini, and smoke cigars. We all have our vices, right?" He laughed heartily. "Anyway, last week his FSB contact asked if he'd heard of the case of this Russian arms dealer, illegally imprisoned—his American lawyer used the word "entrapment" —for smuggling weapons. He's been in a federal prison. The station chief said he hadn't but that he'd look into it. And so here we are. For several complicated reasons, no US government official can be a party to such a deal, at least at this end. And the Nuncio cannot be involved, at least not yet. So, we need your help. Let's you and I take a walk and go meet somebody."

The went up an elevator to a special office, featuring locks, entry codes, and soft jazz muzak. It sounded like Diana Krall. Nice.

The Ambassador pressed a code, a buzzer rang, and he walked into the office. "Father Ishmael, allow me to introduce you to Daniel, our CIA station chief. Gentlemen, I must now leave, as I have another meeting at the Foreign Ministry. We must brief the Russians on the President's upcoming visit. Thank you, Father, we'll be in touch."

The Fat Man

Daniel was shy, but exuded warmth and had a wry smile. His handshake was soft, even a bit squishy. He was a long-time 'Russia hand,' legendary for his recruitment and handling of some of the most sensitive agents in Cold War history. He was an enormous man, weighing well over 350 pounds, and wore a white suit, spats, and large-framed glasses, his balding pink head shiny when he removed his yarmulke. He looked like a morbidly obese version of George Smiley, had George Smiley been a Jew.

The Fat Man had served in Russia for nearly fifteen years and spoke the language fluently in his child-like, squeaky voice. He had paid his way through graduate school by doing magic tricks, making things disappear. Father Ishmael wondered how he had passed surveillance school. The man was Pickwickian, huffing and puffing even when walking across the larger office to his small private office. He even took a few puffs from his inhaler.

After seating himself behind his desk, he told Father Ishmael a story. Once, at a reception, he'd taken a GRU general's star off his shoulder-boards—right in front of his eyes—and presented it back to him in a tumbler of chilled vodka, in effect recreating the shocked general's promotion ceremony, in which the newly-minted officer had to down the vodka, catching the star between his teeth. Only then would be a true General.

Was there a moral to this story? Ishmael wondered.

As if reading his mind, the old magician warned him: "Don't try to be too sneaky with the Russians! Ha!"

Father Ishmael had learned years ago, don't underestimate fat guys. When he was in the military, one of the best teachers was an obese martial artist. He looked like a walrus, and waddled and moved like one, everything about him slow. Until you pointed a gun or knife in his face, and it would disappear in a flash, only to be pointed at your throat. He was a walrus, okay, but a mean, fast walrus. Not to be messed with.

"First off, Father, thank you for helping us. You've been briefed by the Nuncio and the Ambassador. We need your help on this kidnapping case, and a possible trade. But it's a bit more complicated than your normal exchange. There's another party. The Russians have a material witness, who is wanted by the Hague Tribunal for questioning regarding the Srebrenica massacre in Bosnia in 1995 of more than 7,000 Muslim men, women, and children. I know about Srebrenica because I served as station chief in Sarajevo during that time. The Russians—we're sure of this—had Russian military officers embedded there as observers and advisors. The one we know about is a former Spetsnaz and GRU officer. We don't know the details, but after multiple tours of duty, he quit, and was given a pension, and re-settled under an assumed name and fake visa in the U.S. He worked as a school bus driver in Dallas, Texas. Then one day, he simply vanished into thin air. He didn't show up for work or call in. Shortly before that, a routine audit at INS had flagged his visa for review. He disappeared the next day. We have signals intercepts suggesting he was warned. We want to add him to the trade, along with the priest and the Russian arms dealer. We're certain he's back in Russia. We're looking for him, but we want you to find him, and make an approach. We'll take care of the rest. We think he's hiding in a monastery, probably near Moscow, such as Sergeyev Posad, where his old GRU handler can meet with him and bring him the odd care package. Here's a photo; please look at it, memorize it, and give it back to me."

Ishmael accepted the photo and examined it while the station chief went on.

"I'd like for you to meet with the FSB liaison to discuss the matter of the priest and the swap. Do not mention the other elements of trade until we can confirm the other Russian's identity and location. We're still not 100% sure that he's alive, okay? If the FSB finds out about him, they are likely to take matters into their own hands. They play rather dirty and will happily neutralize this possible material witness. If it became public knowledge that Russia had official GRU officers embedded in Bosnian Serb units, it could be very problematic for them. Father, this situation is very, very delicate and at the highest level of security clearance. There is a lot more that I cannot say at this time. Your role is rather critical here. Be careful."

Sarajevo

The Fat Man had told Ishmael everything they knew about Yuri, which admittedly was not much.

"He arrived in Bosnia in January, 1995. He was initially assigned as a military attaché at the Russian Embassy, but later transferred to be an observer with a Bosnian Serb military unit. He had previously served in Afghanistan and, later, in Chechnya. He had requested the transfer after his wife and young child, who had been living on base near Grozny, were killed in a terrorist attack. (He was also injured in the assault and walks with a limp.) After a few months of studying the Bosnian language, his transfer was approved. Besides his limp, he wore his grief on his sleeve, and his commanding officer, a Colonel in the GRU, even noted his bereavement and profound sense of loss."

Yuri had simply wanted to get out of Russia, where every place, smell, sight, and memory reminded him of his wife and child. He saw them in his dreams nightly, and prayed for forgiveness, deliverance, and solace. The Jesus Prayer softened his heart, and he'd repeat it—"*Gospodi, pomilui me*"—over and over.

Yuri had grown up a farm boy near a small village outside Moscow. He'd worked hard on the farm, baling hay, playing hockey at school, and practicing boxing. While serving in an Army unit during his required two-year enlistment, his superiors had noticed him. He never complained, and he never quit during an exercise. He smiled and was well-liked by others, escaping the cruelty of Russian military hazing, called *dedovshchina*. One time, a drunken fellow enlisted soldier tried to hit Yuri with a stick and a chain. Yuri quietly disarmed him, threw the stick away, and lashed him to a fence with the chain.

And so it began. One day, an officer wearing no insignia, a ruddy, handsome-looking chap, stopped by to observe the division's exercises. He spotted Yuri and invited him to have a drink. He told Yuri, "We need young men like you. We're part of the elite unit called Spetsnaz, and I believe that you'd do very well. The training is rigorous. You can decline if you wish. Most of our prospective soldiers fail these tests. That's okay, we welcome all tryouts. But I have observed you. You're a hard-working farm boy. Your parents are good Communists, and they served the Motherland with distinction. Your Dad fought at Stalingrad."

Yuri's first thought was, *What? How do they know that?* Dad never spoke of the war. His Mom was a nurse. She too had served on the Belorussian front, that's how they met when Dad was wounded. But he knew precious little about that. Except for Victory Day parades and movies on TV, families rarely spoke of the Great Patriotic War, in which over 20 million Soviet citizens had perished.

Training started the next day. Yuri and his fellow recruits would run several miles at a time, including to breakfast, lunch, and dinner. They performed thousands of pushups, sit-ups, deep knee bends, and rolls. All while carrying their weapon. "Run boys, run! Relax your muscles, keep the guns over your heads, smile, and sing! Faster!" It wasn't hard; it was just like the Army, right? But after a few weeks, it changed. They brought in a Spetsnaz officer who was short, stocky, even a bit fat. Several candidates were given a knife or stick and told to attack him. They did so. Yuri remembered how much it hurt later. The guy's hands were like sledgehammers—boom, boom, boom! He remembered getting whacked with his own stick, and cut—just enough to bleed, not to kill—and poked with his knife.

Then the teachers blindfolded him and the other candidates, coming at them with sticks, knives, Cossack whips, and chains. He was covered in welts, as each contact burst every capillary. But when he thought, *I've made it, it's done*—"Not so fast, Yuri." Each candidate had to fight a large, wild dog with only a short stick. The dog was large, fierce, and fast. The dog bit him on the leg, and he screamed. He beat him with the stick, over and over until he could grab the dog, and choke him out. The instructor said, "We are all like wild dogs. We are members of a pack, and the pack abhors weakness. We want you to be a dog, or a wolf. Like Lenin said, When living among wolves, howl like a wolf."

For the final exam, he was thrown off a speeding train, and told, run, escape, and make it back to this base near Moscow by next week. If you get caught or turn yourself in, it's over. He was given a knife, that was all. It was winter and bitterly cold. The Russians love the cold—who doesn't cherish the first snowfall or waking up to a morning frost? Yuri didn't know how he survived. He slept in haylofts, killed farm animals, ate raw meat, and traveled only at night, mostly through forests and bogs. He saw wild boars, and for several days, a large female bear and her cubs followed him. A week later, frostbitten, dangerously dehydrated, and suffering diarrhea, he arrived at the base.

The Colonel was waiting, and he smiled, hugged Yuri, and greeted him. "Thank God you made it, I'm so happy." Both shed a tear as they drank a vodka toast and embraced, like brothers.

After that, the GRU came calling. He was interviewed by an old, frumpy, overweight Colonel. They talked over hot tea.

The Colonel began his pitch by saying, "The GRU is different from the SVR or FSB. We are proud patriots, and our organization is characterized by boldness, courage, strength, and humility. Our officers serve in the most challenging environments, often under deep cover, including as illegals. It is important to change your psyche and your body language. You are not a soldier! You will be a diplomat, an attaché, a student, or a businessman. You must be relaxed and not show any tension. None at all! For diplomats are not tense, they are calm. We search for officers with friendly smiles, people skills, and likeability. We will teach you foreign languages. It could be French, German, English, Chinese, Spanish, or Arabic. Your former Colonel in Spetsnaz is fluent in Spanish. Welcome to the organization."

Training was rigorous, and involved tradecraft, surveillance, foreign language study, and other diplomatic skills. All tattoos were erased with visits to a dermatologist, whose laser removed all insignias from the airborne units or Spetsnaz. He was sent on area-familiarization trips, to see if he'd attract the attention of local police, immigration, or counterintelligence. He spent two months in Belgrade as a tourist, and was told, "Just walk around, have fun, eat good food, and keep a low profile." He enjoyed the Serbs. They were good fun, and knew how to make merry, with eating, drinking, feasting, and singing. One of his pals was very good at chess, and would play for hours, taking an extra drink per game. (Somehow the guy actually improved with each match!) The Serbian girls were delightful, but he kept his distance, his natural reserve re-emerging.

And so, he eventually found himself outside of Sarajevo, in July 1995. He was attached to Bosnian Serb military unit. They went to a town named Srebrenica. In the days before, General Ratko Mladić, commander of the Bosnian Serb Army, had visited. He played chess with his troops, shared a drink and cigarette, and smiled for photos. He was a jovial man, whose smile hid his sense of tragedy, hate, and loss. The year prior, his beloved daughter, a medical student at the University of Belgrade, had killed herself in shame over her father's actions during the Bosnian war; she had been dating a Muslim boy. General Mladić never got over it, his loss, his hatred of what this war had done to his country.

That day, Yuri knew that something was wrong. Buses came, loading up and taking away thousands of Bosnian civilians, many men, but also women and children. General Mladić had greeted them, smiling, and promising them safety. He hugged babies, and gently touched the cheeks of the mothers. But Yuri saw something else. He saw the fear in the civilians, and he knew. He had seen this same fear in Afghanistan and in Chechnya, during his prior military service.

He stepped away and called the Colonel on a satellite phone. "It's going down, Colonel. They're going to kill them all. I saw the bulldozers, for digging of mass graves. Please, Colonel, stop it. Call Mladić, call it off."

"I'm sorry," his superior officer replied. "We're only there to observe and to advise, and only if and when requested."

And then the buses were gone, leaving only the empty fields.

When the soldiers returned, they were covered in blood, human gore, and semen, for some had jerked off or raped the Muslim women before and after shooting them. Oh, Lord have mercy, how they sang, wept, laughed, and drank *slivovica*, Serbian plum brandy. They toasted each other and cheered when Bosnian Serb President Dr. Radovan Karadžić gave a speech on the radio, saying, "I gave the order for the operation in Srebrenica, and as commander-in-chief, I am pleased with the result."

The Serb soldiers backslapped each other and howled like wolves. They wept, hugged each other, and danced all night. "*Samo Sloga Srbina Spasava*! Fuck the Muslims and their Turk whores!" On and on it went.

Yuri radioed the Colonel, and said, "I need to come to the embassy to file a cable."

"That's fine, see you tomorrow."

The next morning, the Colonel greeted him, wearing a suit, and offering him a coffee and a *burek* pastry. Sarajevo was quiet that morning, and seeing something different in Yuri's eyes, the Colonel suggested a walk through the old town, down Ferhadija. He had often walked downtown, stopping in the quaint cafés to sip a Turkish coffee, eat sweets, and take in the morning—all in a beautiful, ancient city that seemed, in many ways, to have disappeared overnight.

It was hard not to appreciate the Sarajevans' love of their city, their sheer pleasure in a daytime stroll. One could, while walking, veer a few blocks off to the Principov Most—the historic bridge spanning the Miljacka River—where the Serb nationalist Gavrilo Princip had fatally wounded Archduke Franz Ferdinand and his wife, setting ablaze the powder-keg of World War I. Like the Sarajevans, Yuri appreciated its aromas of sweat, cigarette smoke, sweets, onions, garlic, perfume, and coffee. But he despaired over the city's tragedy and suffering.

As they walked by the old synagogue, the Colonel told him the Mossad's version of Sarajevo's tale—how its brave officers and agents would— by trading weapons to the Bosnian Serbs—'exfiltrate' its long-standing Jewish community and smuggle out its precious artifacts and cultural treasures. Sarajevo had always been a multi-ethnic, multi-religious—Serb Orthodox, Muslim, Jewish, and Croat Catholic—*civitas*, with a heritage of tolerance and cultural porosity. But how could Yuri or the Colonel—like the Sarajevans—have foreseen what Radovan Karadžić—psychiatrist, poet, Bosnian Serb political leader—had written, prophetically and from the depths of his unconscious, in 1968? Karadžić often sang on his gusle, his eerie, prescient revelations looking into the future and seeing Sarajevo ablaze, destroyed, fearful, and bereft of memory. That Sarajevo—which belonged to so many—would disappear and be gone forever. Would Yuri ever see its streets once again full, its cafés a lodestone for those seeking solace, companionship, laughter, and romance? Would he hear the sounds of the muezzin, its haunting call to prayer? He thought of the politicians who'd created this war: Slobodan Milošević, Dr. Radovan Karadžić, and Alija Izetbegović—whose dream of a pure Bosnian Islamic state fueled Bosnia's separatist ambitions, along with his pro-Iranian revolutionary colleagues carrying the SDA's banner.

Yuri found himself weeping on that same Ottoman bridge, where Gavrilo Princip had fired his fateful rounds—or, in Radovan Karadžić's words, those "wonderful, majestic bullets."

"Colonel," he said, "I can't do this anymore."

The Colonel touched Yuri's cheek gently, wiped his tears away, and upon returning to their office, signed Yuri's transfer orders.

Texas

The Colonel had used his influence to get Yuri retired for medical reasons. He saw the pain, the hurt, and the damage of the thousand-yard stare. He had seen it in Afghanistan many times, as a young Spetsnaz officer. He'd seen the killing and the tortures. He'd seen the dead, the mutilated, flayed, and desecrated bodies, often charred black. He never forgot those smells. Sometimes it was better to die.

Like one of the Colonel's instructors had told him, "I always carry a second grenade in combat, with the pin off." The Colonel had seen what the Mujahedeen could do, both to their Afghan, as well as Russian enemies. He remembered the time when their unit rescued a captive Spetsnaz soldier. He was bleeding, and had been raped, with his balls cut off, and stuffed in his mouth. They had carved 'Allahu Akhbar' on his chest. What fucking animals. It made killing them easy.

Knowing these things, the Colonel, who had a kind heart and affection for Yuri, signed his papers. And he did more, supplying his ex-officer with a job, a false passport, and a green card.

Yuri found himself in Dallas, where he lived quietly in a tiny apartment near a park and drove a school bus. The children's voices and laughter brought him cheer and joy, even a bit of peace. It was good life, and he began to heal. He quietly attended nearby

71

Orthodox Services (his passport was from Bosnia), and this too brought comfort and solace.

Nothing last forever, though. One day, he arrived at work, only to find out that an immigration agent had been by, asking for lists of all employees. Yuri didn't know this, but they were looking for illegal Mexican workers, or workers with fake visas. Unlike his usual self, Yuri panicked and made a phone call to a coded number to Moscow.

"They're on to me, colonel. I've got to get out. I will follow the protocol."

What Yuri couldn't know, was that the NSA had pinged the number. They couldn't break the code, but their analyst wondered, Why in the name of God is a local call from a Dallas school bus depot being made to a GRU general in Moscow? They notified the FBI, who said, "Sure, we're on it."

Of course, during that time, the FBI had other priorities, such as hostage-takings, cults, and Mafia cases in New York. Opening an investigation in Dallas would have to wait a few days. Yuri vanished, following an emergency exfiltration protocol that the colonel and he had discussed. Yuri did not yet know of the colonel's promotion to general, but he knew what to do. He hitchhiked to the Hill Country, where there was a small Russian monastery, Christ of the Hills, famous for its vineyards and icon-making. A contact there, Father Sergei, could help. It was a quiet, serene place outside Blanco, and the Hill Country was gorgeous. He arrived in spring, and the wildflowers were in bloom. Yuri liked bluebonnets. It all reminded him of summers on the Volga, of swimming, fishing, and watching the stars.

No, they would never find him here. He would wait.

The general had already departed Moscow for Houston, flying in disguise and on a fake Canadian passport. He had served in Madrid and spoke perfect Spanish, as well as fluent English. He was going to Houston to attend a conference on biomedical ethics. ("You have a prisoner, soldier. Do you cut his hand off with your shovel to make him talk? Or stick it up his ass? What would *you* do, soldier?") Oh yes, he knew ethics, first-hand.

But the general never quite made it to the conference. He rented a car and headed for Blanco. He wore a cassock, cross, and looked like an exact replica of an Orthodox priest on a visit to the monastery to meet with penitents. Upon his arrival, he noticed the bluebonnets and had a message delivered to Father Sergei. He left a bluebonnet in the front office.

Yuri saw him first and limped over to him, where they embraced.

"Come now Yuri, we must go quickly."

They arrived at the Mexican border several hours later, after a quick meal of fajitas in Laredo, where they had spent the night, crossing the next morning. For several hours, their drive took them through Juan Rulfo's Mexico, a beautiful and desolate part of the Chihuahuan desert. There were thousands of huge, towering cacti, along with yucca plants and ocotillos. This was the Mexico of fables, dreams, and imagination.

The general told Yuri stories about Mexico, its people, culture, and food. He spoke of its great writers such as Juan Rulfo, Octavio Paz, and Carlos Fuentes. He spoke of its artists, Orozco, Rivera, Kahlo, and Tamayo. He spoke as if they were real and alive, for even though he had never met them, they were friends in spirit: wanderers and journeymen. The General had been to Mexico City twice while serving as an interpreter for the visiting Minister of Defense. But he also knew that Mexico City was crawling with CIA and other allied services. He and Yuri would have to be careful.

What he didn't know is that NSA had picked up a coded call from a remote monastery in central Texas. What did it mean? Again, the FBI was notified, but this time they told NSA, "We'll get to it."

The general knew they'd have to be careful from here on. Traveling in disguise, he and Yuri, again changing passports, boarded an Aero Mexico flight to Havana.

Havana

The stayed in a safe house near the Old City. But they still needed to exercise caution, for Cuban counterintelligence—although 'friendly' and trained by the KGB—nevertheless spied on them too. And the Cubans were nothing if not professional.

The general tipped their minder well, buying him a mojito at the classic art-deco Hotel Nacional, where they could mingle with European tourists, enjoy a rum and a Montecristo cigar. After all, they were traveling as European tourists, right? Should they not hide in plain sight and act as such? This was something that the general had learned long ago, when he completed GRU training at The Aquarium.

By nightfall, they had secured reservations at a local *palabar*, one of many small, family-owned garden restaurants that served excellent seafood. By the time they departed for their safehouse, the general had made new friends, and was frolicking with the local girls, dancing with the tourists, and singing German, Spanish, and French drinking songs. Ah, the general, always the life of the party.

The next day before their evening flight, they walked along the Malecon, passing the US Interests Section, with its hundreds of black Cuban patriotic flags blocking the view from the street. The afternoon found them and their minder wandering in Old Havana, marveling at its enchanting beauty, and savoring drinks at the famous Ambos Mundos, where Hemingway would share a drink with his NKVD minder while cavorting with the local girls.

Yuri remained mostly silent, and he let the general, ever the social butterfly, do all the talking. Their day ended with a trip to, and private tour of, the Cohiba cigar factory. Havana was enchanting, but Yuri continued to feel out of sorts. He could not relate to the general's joie de vivre. He even found himself wondering, What would Russia be like? How would he adapt? He had not been in Russia for several years. He had read about how much it had changed under Yeltsin, and the oligarchs, with their excesses and wealth. He didn't know what to think, or where he belonged. He hadn't spoken Russian in several years, and he had no family left in Russia, for his parents had died a few years prior to his deployment to Bosnia. He worried about all this, and it made him nauseated, so he chewed antacids and brooded.

The general also said little as they went to the airport. He brooded too, worried about the FSB. Would they catch on to Yuri?

The Watcher

He didn't exist. He was a ghost, part of a novel program at CIA, that had borrowed from, and expanded upon, the better-known counterintelligence surveillance program at the FBI. The chief difference was that the CIA's professional watchers all worked overseas. They never went near an embassy, and they never approached potential targets or persons of interest. They simply watched people.

The Watcher had also spent a night in Laredo, while the general and Yuri were there. And like them, he too, drove to Mexico City. He followed them and tracked them during their visit. He took photos, like a tourist. He had tracked the general for several years, ever since the latter's time in Bosnia. He knew the general, he knew his daily rhythms, his body language. But he did not know his voice. Others did that and attempted to listen in on his conversations. But he knew the GRU man's facial expressions, his smiles, his frowns, his eyes, and his laugh. He had seen the wrinkles on his forehead, the worries, and the furrowed brow. And so he had watched as the general and Yuri boarded their plane to Havana. Why were they going to Havana? Why not just take a direct flight home to Moscow? Who was the stranger with him? He was clearly not a diplomat or a known intelligence officer. Why was he traveling with the general? The general always traveled alone.

The Watcher took his photos, knowing that CIA Headquarters would sort it out. He boarded the Aeroflot flight home to Moscow, assuming that time would tell. Regardless, he'd be in Moscow by the time the General landed.

The Watcher's small, elite unit tracked Russian, Iranian, North Korean, Chinese, and Syrian intelligence officers, diplomats, and other persons of interest around the world. Some of them were based in Washington, DC, while others—such as the Watcher— lived overseas. He had been in Moscow for two years, where he taught part-time at a local international school.

The Watcher didn't exist. He had been recruited from another specialized unit: the US Customs Patrol Office of Investigation, known as the Shadow Wolves. He was Navajo and had grown up poor on the Rez. His father had farmed, and his mother raised sheep while caring for the family. He and his brother had grown up outdoors, tracking animals, hunting, and hiking, as taught by their father, who was also a medicine man, or shaman, within their tribe.

His grandfather had been a code talker in World War II. His father had been a very quiet, serious person. He'd taught his brother and him to track animals, including blindfolded and at night. The Watcher had come to understand animals and their ways. He'd learned to live off the land too, and as a young man, had hiked the entire Grand Canyon, with only a knife as gear. Like the legendary hiker and writer Colin Fletcher, he too had walked through time. In the bowels of the canyon, he recalled being dehydrated as he approached the waters of the Colorado River. He had begun hallucinating, and no longer knew what was real. He drank the water, weeping joyously, his hands cupping it, like a supplicant's.

But as a Navajo, a Dine, he had always felt slightly lost in the world of the white man. Therefore, he'd forced himself to go beyond his comfort zone and enrolled at ASU, where he'd studied Hindi and Urdu. He became a Shadow Wolf after a Customs Agency recruiter visited the campus and passed his name along to the right people. The Watcher got noticed not so much because of his tracking abilities, but because of his language skills. Later, when recruited by CIA, he achieved exceptional scores on their language assessment tests. So, off he went to Russian language school for a year, and then his Moscow posting began.

His sole job was to track the general. He knew his daily routine and had driven through his neighborhood at Sparrow Hills. He knew the general's walks, when the general would go with his wife and daughter to the overlook near MGU, Moscow State University. Like the general, he couldn't get enough of the shimmering of Moscow's lights at night, like an earthbound galaxy. It reminded him of the desert stars back home.

He had driven to GRU headquarters, where the General worked, for the Watcher could pass as an Uzbek fast-food cook at a local stand where the SVR officers ate on good-weather days. Like a true Russian, the Watcher came to love smells of the woods, the ubiquitous white birches, and the feel of first snow on a winter morning.

It puzzled him when the general didn't drive to work at Yasenevo one day, but instead took the Metro to a neighborhood near the airport. The general used a lengthy, detailed surveillance-detection route, switching trains, getting off and back on the Metro, buying a snack at a kebab stand, chatting with the various locals, and moving, always moving, not quickly, but still moving. *Damn, he's good*, thought the Watcher. *One of the best.*

But the Watcher was also good. He blended in by wearing a leather jacket, cap, and boots, like your ordinary working man, now tailing the General around a small lake, where old men fished, bottles of cheap vodka by their sides.

He could not contain his amazement when the General came to a small apartment block and entered the building. The Watcher could barely see who answered, but he knew when the door opened wider and the General embraced Yuri. It was a pretty day, so they both went outside, sat on a bench for an hour or so, laughing, chatting, and feeding the ducks at the pond. They looked like two old friends catching up on old times.

In his coded radio report the next day, the Watcher requested permission to track Yuri as well. The answer came back quickly: "No, just focus on the General."

FSB

Father Ishmael had received a phone call telling him that the FSB liaison officer, a colonel named Misha, wished to meet with him. A car waited that morning to take him to a FSB safe house. He got in, not knowing what to expect. The driver spoke little English, but he knew exactly where to go. Upon arrival at the safe house, Father Ishmael found himself in a small courtyard, where a door suddenly opened and Misha came out to greet him.

"Thank you, Father, for coming. We have much to discuss. But let's have tea and some Russian snacks—*zakuski*—first. They're quite delicious. And we must toast to our new friendship."

In a nondescript apartment, the colonel poured two tiny shot glasses filled the FSB's own limited-edition vodka. Ishmael tossed his down and found himself surprised. Wow, it was smooth…like silk: soft and delicate.

"Your reputation precedes you," said Misha. "We know of your work in numerous kidnapping and hostage cases in Mexico. The SVR Rezident in Mexico City is an old friend, as we both started in the KGB together. He's told me all about you. We'd like for you to help us with a situation. It's a bit delicate. For some odd reason, CIA—I know about your visit with the fat guy—and your Embassy, as well as the Nuncio, want you to assist us with this situation. I'm a bit puzzled why CIA or the Ambassador, or even the Nuncio, can't handle this, as it's an easy trade. Our illegally imprisoned Russian citizen for an American spy, who claims to be a priest. I am puzzled as to why they are assigning this negotiation to you, an American priest now living in Moscow. I respect your work in Mexico City, Father Ishmael. But why you now? Why are you here? This is all a bit odd and strange. Maybe you're not a real priest either. Why are you in Russia? What are you doing in Moscow?"

Misha didn't look the part of an FSB officer. He was tall, ruddy, and had a goatee, as well as a ponytail. His hair was graying a bit, as he was in his late 50s. He wore nice slacks, black loafers, a conservative tie, and a black leather jacket. To Father Ishmael, he looked like a German filmmaker. This was ironic, as Misha had served in an undercover role in Berlin, where he had overseen the hunting and elimination of Chechen terrorists.

"We want to do a trade, Father. It's as simple as that, so let's keep it simple. Tell the Fat Man, the Nuncio, and your ambassador to make it happen. You and I can coordinate the transfer. Tell them we'll do the transfer at the Vienna airport. We have excellent contacts there and will manage the handoff. You're free to go, Father. Please be careful, though. I have placed a great deal of my prestige on the line. There are many in the FSB who oppose *any* trade with the Americans. For they—and even you, Father—are the main enemy, the *Glavni Vrag.*"

Father Ishmael smiled and nodded, acknowledging the warning. "I have a request for you, in order that you might be of assistance in this case. I need to visit the imprisoned priest. I need to meet with him, pray with him, and offer him the Holy Eucharist. And most of all, Colonel, I need proof of life."

Misha stared at him, his eyes not giving away his thoughts. He touched his palms to his forehead, then turned and said, "Very well, Father, let me think about it. I will give you my answer within 24-48 hours."

What Father Ishmael, the Ambassador, and the station chief didn't know was that Misha was also aware of Yuri. He had long wondered, who was this guy, who came from Havana? What was he doing there? He had last been in Russia in 1995, a few years prior, then vanished. Who was he? And why was a high-ranking GRU general traveling with him from Havana, and even going to his apartment in Moscow? The *rezidentura* in Havana had no knowledge of the general's trip. Misha didn't like ambiguity or patterns that made no sense. They made him worried and nervous and took his sleep. His ulcers even acted up. He had a file that showed Yuri had been in the Army, then Spetsnaz, but after that, nothing. The file had been sanitized and wiped clean. He considered approaching the general, but he knew that the GRU played even dirtier and rougher than the FSB. Misha was only a colonel, and he lacked the status or rank to directly approach the general. He could conceivably make an approach via his superiors, but that carried risk. Any investigation of a general, especially a high-ranking GRU general, required high levels of approval. For now, Misha knew that this wasn't likely. *Be patient*, he told himself. *Be patient, wait, and watch.*

The Jew

There was another person aware of Yuri and the General. Moshe was a Jew, and a Serbian Jew, to boot. He had grown up in Belgrade and had made *aliyah* as a teen. Moshe didn't exist. In Moscow, he was completely invisible. He had been sent there temporarily, pulled away from his routine duties in the Hague, where he served as an investigator for the International Criminal Tribunal. But what the Hague didn't know about Moshe was that he was a deep-cover Mossad agent, embedded in the ICTY. He had also served in Bosnia, where he had exfiltrated hundreds of Jews, who had, like their forebears, lived in Sarajevo for centuries. He had also coordinated the operation which saved the Haggadah, one of Judaism's holiest and most sacred texts, from the Synagogue in Sarajevo before the Serb militias had bombed and looted it. For this, he had received kudos and awards, both within Mossad and from the Prime Minister. He had been an observer in Tel Aviv when the exfiltrated Jews landed, and had wept, kissed the ground, thanking God for His benevolence and mercy, and for allowing his people safe passage to Israel.

Moshe had developed sources in Sarajevo and, later, while working at the Hague; he had seen Russian soldiers embedded in Bosnian Serb military units. But as close as he got, he couldn't get a name. He wondered if it was true, or if he were only imagining things. He had interviewed many survivors of Srebrenica, and he realized that they were so traumatized by grief, loss, sorrow, and, yes, even hate, that their memories could get mixed up. The mind, especially a traumatized one, could trick one to believe whatever it wanted.

His only evidence was a grainy photo of a soldier, who appeared to have a Russian insignia and walked with a limp. The soldier had vanished into thin air, and the GRU *resident* at the time, now a general based in Moscow, had also disappeared shortly thereafter. Moshe didn't believe in such coincidences. But both trails had gone quiet. Until now.

Mossad had received—through an intercept from Unit 8200—a coded radio call from the GRU general's office in Moscow, to a monastery in Texas. And then one of its agents in Texas had noticed the general's presence in Houston, and later in Mexico City. He was traveling with another person—who the hell was he?—and got on a plane together from Havana to Moscow.

What was going *on*?

When the general made his first visit to Yuri's apartment, Moshe was watching and wondering, who the hell is he visiting? Moshe immediately noticed that the host had a limp. Could this be the same Russian soldier from Srebrenica?

Moshe flew back to Tel Aviv, where he met with the Mossad director in charge of operations. The director thanked him and told him, "Be patient, we will find this out. We may have to tell the Americans, but only if and when the timing is right. If we or they act hastily, the Russian soldier will vanish, and so might the general. We know that the FSB is also looking into the general's activities. It is never good to hurry in such situations, Moshe. Patience is a virtue, right?"

The General's Secret

What nobody knew, except for the Fat Man and one or two of his superiors at CIA headquarters, was that the general harbored a deep secret. Or he didn't, but his wife did. The general had been married for more than 25 years. His work had often taken him far away, to far-flung corners of the earth, many of them less hospitable than others. Over the years, their moves and his travels had taken a toll on his wife. They had met when he attended GRU training at the Aquarium. She was a simple person, who had attended university, studying Spanish. She worked as a bank teller, and occasionally as a translator. She was pretty, with blue eyes, and a gentle nature. She smiled easily and liked to read. She was the general's muse. They had a daughter, now grown and a student at Moscow State University, where she studied languages. They had traveled together, lived abroad, and gone on vacations all over Europe. Her favorite cities were Barcelona, Paris, Mallorca, Venice, and Rome. For some odd reason, her soul seemed more Mediterranean than Russian.

After the general's tour in Bosnia, his wife changed. She became more withdrawn and no longer found joy in things. She stopped reading and quit her job. She spent most of the day in bed and wouldn't shower or put on makeup for days on end. She and the general never touched, and she had taken to sleeping in a separate bedroom. Their walks on the banks of the Moscow River ceased.

When he arrived home after a long day at Yasenevo—and given his rank and obligations, his days were often very long—her eyes would be dark and reddened from crying. The general worried about her, a lot, and didn't know what to do. He feared she might become suicidal. For the first time in his life, his personal and professional skills failed him.

He thought of having her see a physician at a private clinic, but she refused. There was no question of having her see a specialist at the military clinic used by senior GRU officials. This was out of the question, and in the system in which he labored, career suicide. His enemies in the FSB and GRU would use this against him. So, he did the unthinkable. He reached out to the Americans. He left a message with the Fat Man, whom he knew to be their station chief.

Meeting in Moscow was totally out of the question. The general suggested Vienna, where they could meet more freely, and he could escape the withering surveillance. A week later, he found himself in Vienna, where he had gone on the pretext of attending a routine meeting at the GRU *rezidentura*. He had an extra hour of free time in the morning, and found himself sitting on a bench near Stadtpark, wearing a disguise and walking a Schnauzer. He looked like a regular, old Austrian pensioner walking his dog in the morning. *Grüß Gott*, he said to passerby. He fed the ducks well until he saw the Fat Man waddling toward him.

The American asked—in perfect German—if the seat on the bench was free. *Naturlich*. The Fat Man was wearing an Austrian loden suit, and a Tiroler hat with a feather. He had mutton-chop whiskers, making him look like a Fiacker driver. Even his Fiacker carriage was parked nearby.

He said to the general, "Would you like to see the Innerestadt? How about a Fiacker ride? You can bring your dog too."

"*Sehr gut.* How *gemutlichkeit.*"

They spoke a little longer, making arrangements for their next meeting in Vienna. The general would bring his wife along, and they'd do some shopping, see a museum or two, and take a walk along the Danube. He hoped that a change of pace and scenery would lift her spirits.

But the Fat Man knew what the general didn't. After hearing the painful story of his wife's suffering, the Fat Man had said, in Russian, in his softest voice, "I will help you general. This one's on me, no strings attached. It's a human thing, and the right thing to do. We will, you and I, together, help your wife. You will get your wife back."

Upon his return to Moscow, the Fat Man had asked to speak to the embassy's psychiatrist. He was part of a worldwide team, scattered regionally around the globe, that served the mental health needs of embassies and consulates, caring for diplomats, their family members, and the foreign nationals who worked in the embassy. The embassy psychiatrist had served in Moscow for nearly two years. He was taken aback when the Fat Man asked for a meeting, for he'd had few dealings with the CIA station.

The psychiatrist looked a little different from your average staffer: he wore black jeans, boots, and a black leather jacket, which he had bought from a Chechen jacket dealer at a local *rynok*.

He asked the Fat Man, "Why me? It's delicate, and if the Russians find out, I'll get kicked out of the country."

"No worries," the Fat Man replied. He had not told the psychiatrist who the general was, only that he was a high-ranking Russian diplomat. But the psychiatrist had figured that out already. "We'll do this in Vienna, it's safer there. The ambassador has been briefed on a need-to-know basis, and he approves. You ask, why me? Because you happen to speak fluent Russian, that's why. And because the patients whom you've cared for at our embassy—please don't be shocked, Doc, for there are few secrets here—speak well of you. I don't know much about psychiatry, but I know a good doctor when I see one. And you know Russia, you're comfortable with the culture.

The psychiatrist shrugged away the flattery and sighed, knowing he had little choice but to join this risky venture.

"Thanks," said the Fat Man, rising with effort. "We really appreciate your help on this one, Doc."

The psychiatrist wondered about this. Such work puzzled and intrigued him. So different from his previous work. He had spent years working in jails, prison clinics, and had served as an expert witness in countless courtrooms. Mental illness was the coin of the realm, but so too was Evil. He remembered interviewing a mother who had butchered her children, blinding one of them, a small girl.

After establishing what rapport he could, the doctor had asked her, "What happened to her eyes? What did you do?"

When she began weeping, he knew.

"I ate them," she said, sobbing.

He touched her hand gently. "You're sorry now, right? But you can't take it back, can you?"

She howled and sobbed for a long time, the two of them sitting together in that dank, filthy interview room. What *was* Evil? Who was he to judge?

Then there was the murderer who had beaten and raped an old lady, stealing her food stamps and $200 to buy a few days' worth of crack. The murderer looked mean and had shifty, creepy eyes. A jackal adorned with teardrop tattoos. But his evil and meanness hid his own traumas. One day, in the jail shower, he had been viciously beaten, concussed, and raped. He told the psychiatrist about the attack (which was documented in the medical record), of anal and rectal tears, internal bleeding, and a sexually transmitted disease acquired while being forced to perform oral sex on his tormentors during the rapes. He wept, asking, "Why would anybody do this to me?"

The psychiatrist sat silently, simply listening. The defendant would live, and he ended up not getting the needle. He was an evil person, but he too had suffered, enough. Not a life for a life, but a life worthy of life.

He met the general's wife at a safe house in Vienna. It was comfortable, a small apartment with Jugendstil furniture and tasteful accents. He smiled and introduced himself to his patient.

She looked him in the eye. "I know who you are."

"Oh? How do you know me when we have never met? And how can I be of help?"

After a long silence, she looked up, her eyes no longer downcast, and began to speak. As she did, the psychiatrist recalled something Nathaniel Hawthorne had written: that a person burdened with a secret should especially avoid the intimacy of a physician.

The general's wife spoke of sadness, loss, loneliness, and how her life had lost purpose.

When he asked her, "Do you love your husband?" she burst into tears.

"Of course! I love him, but I'm unworthy of him. He is a good, kind, and generous man. He deserves better than me. His work is busier than ever, as he often works evenings and weekends. He often travels abroad." She sipped her tea and became still.

The psychiatrist had to choose his words carefully, now. Not only was she severely depressed, overwhelmed by the deepest sadness and insecurity, but her isolation was palpable. She was of this world, but also no longer of it.

He spoke more softly, switching to the less formal, more familiar form of address, using her diminutive as well. When he did this, she looked up at him, and he could see tears flowing down her cheeks.

"I will help you, Ninotchka. I will be there for you, and with you. Please allow me to give you your life back. It is a life worthy of you, and a life worth living."

The treatment was straightforward—a trial of an antidepressant. The logistics of getting her the medication were complicated, but the station in Moscow thrived on such challenges, and the Fat Man's logistics experts dived into the details. They did not know who the patient was, but if the Fat Man said do it, they sure as hell did it.

The logisticians were brilliant. One of them was a young, tat-tooed, dread-locked Jamaican-American woman who listened to rap and reggae in the office. She wore black jeans, a Bob Marley dashiki shirt, and colorful jewelry. Before joining the agency, she had worked for a trucking company. She could move mountains and loved nothing more than cracking hard problems.

Follow-up between the psychiatrist and his patient was not an option. But they'd know of her progress through covert communi-cations with the general. The reports after six weeks were encour-aging. The general's wife was slowly getting better. She began to enjoy things, and left the house to go on walks, visit her favorite bookstores such as Dom Knigi, and walked to the Kremlin, passing the Alexander Gardens, with their colorful tulips in spring.

One day the psychiatrist was visiting the GUM Department Store with his family, enjoying window-shopping, and stopping for coffee and blini at one of its many cafés. From a distance, he happened to spot the general's wife. She looked so different that he almost didn't recognize her. She was wearing makeup, a Hermes scarf, and a print dress, and she appeared happy, even radiant. She spotted him staring and gave him a small wave and a smile.

He never saw her again. Nor did the general and the Fat Man meet again. The Fat Man hadn't put a word of this into his cables back home.

It would be their secret.

Lefortovo

A government vehicle with special plates picked Father Ishmael up at his apartment the next morning. He did not know where they were going but suspected that he would at least be allowed to visit the priest in jail. He had no clue as to which prison they'd be going to, but he had worn his cassock, cross, and had brought along a single Holy Communion wafer, along with his Rosary and a Bible. When they arrived at Lefortovo, his heart fluttered, and his chest gave a shudder, for he had heard of its horrors.

He recognized his FSB contact, Misha, at the visitor check-in station. After screening, he was brought to a small, private—as if anything in Russia could be considered private—room. It was spartan, with a small desk and two chairs. The imprisoned priest had clearly suffered plenty of deception, and he eyed Father Ishmael warily. But when Father Ishmael greeted him and held out a Rosary and the Bible, the priest's eyes moistened and he smiled at last.

They prayed the Rosary together. Father Ishmael read that day's readings and offered the priest Holy Communion. *I am the bread of life, he who follows Me shall not hunger.*

Father Ishmael saw that the priest favored one of his legs, and he had scars on his arms from lashings. He also suffered a repeating tremor, his body intermittently shaking, as if from the cold.

His eyes squinted in the light, a sign that he'd been kept in solitary confinement.

Father Ishmael held his hands and, looking him in the eye, said, "Fear not. The Nuncio and American Ambassador sent me. They bring you greetings. We are working on getting you released, but it may take some time. Please be strong, Father, do not lose your faith. Be not afraid! Do you remember those stirring words of Pope John Paul? Shall we recite Psalm 27 together? The Lord is my light and my salvation. Of whom should I be afraid?" He kissed the priest gently on the cheek. "I will be back," he said, and took his farewell.

At that, the priest's countenance changed entirely. "Liar! I'll never be free again. How many pieces of silver did the Russians pay you to betray me?" He spat on Father Ishmael, his eyes wild. "Satan, get thee hence! Guards! Get this false priest out of here! Take me back to my cell!"

Father Ishmael had dealt with strange reactions and powerful emotions in his earlier work with kidnap victims. He had seen victims hug their captors farewell, weeping at the handover. Others would giggle and laugh uncontrollably. Some remained silent with rage, refusing to speak, even when safe, fed, clothed, and reunited with their families. Others were mute, nearly catatonic, rocking back and forth for hours, chanting, humming, crying, and praying, "Forgive me Father, for I have sinned."

Father Ishmael forgave all such reactions. They, like the priest's reaction in Lefortovo, were part of the human condition. As the great Roman philosopher Terence said, "Nothing which is human is alien to me."

Back in Moscow, Father Ishmael briefed the ambassador and the Nuncio. The Fat Man received his report on the session, and even Misha got in touch, inviting Father Ishmael to coffee and *pelmeni* at a café near FSB Headquarters.

At the café, Misha pressed Father Ishmael about the proposed trade. "An easy swap. The priest for the arms dealer." This was the first time that Misha had referred the priest as such, rather than as 'the spy.'"

He told Ishmael that the FSB had briefed the Nuncio and the American Ambassador. So, why the hold-up? Was it due to the FBI? Misha found this puzzling, and he didn't like loose ends. Not that Ishmael could provide any answers.

So, Misha wasn't at all surprised when his superior—an FSB general—told him, "The Americans are holding back. They clearly want more," he said. "So we must wait."

A famous American kidnap negotiator had once written, the hardest part of a hostage negotiation is the wait. But the FSB was accustomed to waiting.

Misha knew about waiting, as he had once worked on a counterintelligence case against the Americans for five long years. He remembered his training at the KGB's First Chief Directorate, at its Red Banner Institute. One of the teachers at the Red Banner Institute had used that unique German word "fingerspitzengefühl," meaning intuitive flair or instinct, which describes exquisite situational awareness and the ability to respond most appropriately to a given situation. This was exactly, Misha realized, what was now needed in this case.

The Monastery

The FSB had Yuri's apartment under passive surveillance. One night, things didn't work so well. Their man drank one too many during his shift and stepped away to the nearby woods to answer a call of nature. When he returned, the lights were still on and the radio playing softly. He could hear the Tchaikovsky Violin Concerto. But Yuri, they would later discover, had vanished.

Fortunately, the Watcher had noted this. The general had driven by in a junky old Lada, which attracted little attention in this proletarian neighborhood. The general was a true genius of disguise. This time, he had dressed up as an old crone, a babushka. He even had the voice and mannerisms right. And so the Watcher had followed them in his Niva, which also did not stand out.

They drove for nearly two hours until they came to Sergeyev Posad, one of Russia's most beautiful and holy of monasteries. Why there? the Watcher wondered.

And then he knew.

The general was helping Yuri disappear. Presently, he would enter the Byzantine labyrinth of Russian Orthodoxy, in which he could vanish eternally.

So, the next day, the Watcher send an urgent, coded radio message to the station, telling them, "He's gone, and we'll soon lose him forever."

Father Ishmael found himself taking a tourist bus to the monastery a few days later, having been briefed by the Ambassador and the Fat Man. His instructions were clear. "ONLY try to verify his identity. You've seen his picture and prior official photo. We only need to know he's there. That way we can make an approach to the general, who can help engineer the complete trade. It's a gamble, as the general's not in on this. Yet. But we think that he might support it, especially as the arms dealer is a former GRU officer, and a close friend of the general."

Father Ishmael appreciated monasteries and churches, for in such places one could truly commune with God. While on vacation from Moscow, he had visited Melk, one of the greatest monasteries in Europe, which sat along the banks of the Danube in lower Austria. He also remembered it as the setting for the monastery in the movie based upon Umberto Eco's novel, *The Name of the Rose*. He remembered how, in the movie, it had burned for days and weeks, its library completely, utterly destroyed. He recalled reading an interview with Eco, in which the author said, "I wrote a novel because I wanted to kill a monk."

Sergeyev Posad was majestic and impressive, with its blue onion domes and white walls. He walked around its expansive interior, stopping to pray and light a candle in each of its chapels. There were icons, including a famous one of Jesus as Pantocrator. Father Ishmael knew little about icons, but he recognized their holiness and intuitively grasped their importance to Russia's Orthodox faith, in which symbol and image meant as much as the Word.

He walked among the tourists, large crowds on that day, as religious holidays were approaching. But there was no sign of Yuri. Until he walked into a gift shop to buy some postcards and thought that he caught a glimpse of Yuri walking in the hallway. But the distance was too great, and he couldn't be sure. The monk could have been Yuri, but he was dressed in a cassock, had graying hair, and a long beard.

Upon his return to Moscow, he briefed the Ambassador and the Fat Man. The latter sent a cable to headquarters, then received permission to deploy the Watcher to Sergeyev Posad. But the instructions remained the same: Only observe and behave naturally.

The Watcher had no diplomatic immunity, and any mishap, or even the tiniest suspicion, would draw the attention of the FSB. For Father Ishmael had reported sensing the intelligence agency's presence on his tail during his trip to the monastery. Hopefully they'd figured him for a religious tourist.

The same would not be the case for the Watcher.

The general felt a welcome sense of calm that month. His wife's health was better, and he had her back. He found himself getting to know her again, including their deep love, based on their many shared memories of their courtship and travels many years ago. They would take walks along the Moscow River, and visit Patriarch's Pond, where they'd sit on benches, watching the birds, the children, and an old man walking his poodle. This made his wife giggle and laugh, as though she were young again, and he too found himself smiling, grateful, and tenderly telling her, "I love you, I love you, you are my world, thank you."

He felt such gratitude that he did something out of character. He covertly sent a postcard to the embassy psychiatrist with a photo of the Kremlin and a single, handwritten word: *spasibo*. As it had no signature or return address, the embassy psychiatrist wondered who could have sent it.

It only took a moment before it clicked. *Of course!* It was his patient, the wife of the Russian official. He took the card to show to the Fat Man, who recognized the general's handwriting, and smiled.

Now, the Fat Man had no reliable or easy way to contact the general. But the Watcher did. One day, the general had taken the Metro from near the Aquarium to a meeting in the Kremlin. On the way back to his main office, he stopped at a local kebab stand. As he paid for his doner kebab, he didn't notice or pay attention to the smelly Uzbek man next to him, arguing in Uzbek with the seller, squabbling that he owed him an extra ruble in change. Nor did the general see the business card slipped into his messenger bag. The card bore a simple message: : *Vienna, Stadtpark, next week.*

The general loved Vienna, its mixture of modernity and tradition. He enjoyed its downtown Innere Stadt, with its charming, delightful coffee shops, gorgeous churches and cathedrals, and many alleyways. He was charmed by the Stadtpark and the Burggarten. Of course, there the city's great museums—the Kunsthistoriches Museum, the Albertina, and the Leopold. He knew the sordid history of the latter, which had acquired most of its art—Klimt, Schiele and Koskoschka—via theft from Vienna's Jewish community during World War II. Or as Sophie Lillie had written, *Was Einmal War.*

Vienna was a city of tragedy, yet also of secrets. The unconscious lurked deep in its psyche. No wonder that Freud had made his greatest discoveries therein, as he had uncovered an entire world of unconscious wishes, hopes, dreams and desires that lay within our minds.

But Vienna also had darker secrets: recruitments, kidnappings, agent meetings, dead drops, and exfiltrations. This too was part of the Schattenstadt, where 50% of the diplomats were thought to be intelligence officers. He had often walked by the large American Embassy, wondering, *What are they thinking? What operations are the CIA plotting behind closed doors?* He wondered about that today.

After a brief meeting with the local GRU station, he resumed his walk, completing a detailed surveillance-detection route throughout the city. He rode the U-Bahn and streetcars. He stopped for a mélange coffee at the famous Café Central. He sat on benches and fed birds. He said hello to strangers, petted their dogs, and said, *Grüß Gott* to passerby. He never saw the Watcher, who had stalked him all day. But when he got to the Stadtpark, he easily spotted the Fat Man, wearing a 3-piece suit with a bowler hat, sipping an espresso and a mineral water and reading the main Viennese daily, *Die Presse.*

"*Bitte schon, kann Ich hier einen sitzplatz nehmen? Jawohl, vielen Dank.*"

Their time together would be short, although the Fat Man's counterintelligence had not seen any evidence of Russian, Austrian, or other surveillance. But they missed the Watcher, dressed up as an old man, walking the Fat Man's Schnauzer and feeding the ducks. And they missed the Jew, wearing his yarmulke, walking slowly with a cane, mumbling, and talking to himself in Yiddish.

The Fat Man said, "Thank you for coming. I'm glad your wife is better. Our psychiatrist is really gifted, and we're grateful that he could be of help to you and your family. Here's a year's worth of medication for her. But, general, please hear me out. We need a favor from you. Our sources have revealed to us that a former Russian soldier—he was a Spetsnaz and GRU officer in Bosnia—whom you know well, is in hiding in Moscow. We have reason to believe that he is in Sergeyev Posad. He is of interest to us, and to the Hague War Crimes Tribunal, as a possible material witness to war crimes at Srebrenica. He could be a critical witness in the prosecutions of General Mladić, Serbia's President Slobodan Milošević, and—once we catch him—the Bosnian Serb leader Dr. Radovan Karadžić. We are proposing that he be added to the trade involving the Russian arms dealer and the American priest being illegally detained in Lefortovo. You and I would broker the trade, and an American priest, who is close to the Nuncio and the imprisoned priest, would be there as a witness. Your man Yuri can be deposed *in camera*, then returned to you and his home in Russia. We know that he means a lot to you, general. You helped him come to America, right? And then when our immigration investigators caught onto him, you flew to Houston to coordinate his repatriation. We know about the drive down to Mexico City and the flight to Havana. Such nice places, right? We'd like to do this quietly, General, without the media. If Interpol were to get involved, everything would leak. The fact that Russia embedded Spetsnaz and GRU officers in the Bosnian Serb

Army would not be taken kindly by the Hague Tribunal, the UN, or frankly, by the international media. I am asking for your help."

The general spoke softly, looking the Fat Man in the eye. "I thank you for coming to meet with me. Vienna is a beautiful city. I always feel the ghost of Harry Lime here, and I can hear the theme song from *The Third Man*…that zither, humming in my ear. Anyway, thank you for your kind offer, and thank you too, for helping my wife. She is much better, and your embassy psychiatrist has rare gifts. She trusts him, as do I. I don't say this lightly. For this I owe you a debt of gratitude." The general cleared his throat. "We'll do the trade here in Vienna. The details can be arranged. The spy for the arms dealer, that part is overt. Because I am a GRU general, and because the arms dealer and I are friends, I am optimistic that the FSB will allow me and my SVR colleague in Vienna to manage the trade. Otherwise, it's best that the FSB not be involved. The other, covert part of the trade, which can be done at the last minute, will involve Yuri, the former Spetsnaz and GRU officer. That part is deeply secret, and nobody must know. Just the two of us. Understood? Please be careful, or you'll get us both killed. And no media, no end-zone dance, as they do in American football. Just a nice, quiet, simple trade."

Tel Aviv

Mossad wondered about this meeting. What was going on? They had photos from their man, the Jew from Sarajevo. But photos couldn't tell what was said, what had been discussed. There was little tension in the men's bodies as they spoke. They relaxed, sipped coffee and mineral water, and smiled often. Only at the end did the General's face turn somber and his countenance stiffen. Why? Was the General defecting? Or acting as an agent-in-place? Or even more ominously, was the Moscow CIA station chief selling secrets to the Russians, to a GRU General? If so, this was explosive.

Was this meeting sanctioned? By whom? The Mossad didn't know, and their man on the ground didn't know either. This made the senior Mossad leaders nervous. They sat around a conference table in Tel Aviv, chewed their fingernails, and sipped on their coffee.

Finally, their director—an elderly, soft-spoken man whose voice was gentle, almost silky in tone—said, "Let us be patient, it will all become clear in due time." He smiled and dismissed them.

He spoke this way because he'd been a psychoanalyst in his previous life. As a case officer, he'd made legendary recruitments: a Hamas leader, a high-ranking Hezbollah terrorist, and a senior Russian GRU officer.

He spotted the Russia branch chief, and remarked, "Nice work. Please give my kindest regards to Moshe. I miss Sarajevo, too."

Misha, Again

The general had already returned to Moscow when his itinerary landed on Misha's desk at FSB a week later. What was he doing in Vienna? The cable suggested that he had had meetings with the GRU *Rezidentura*, but that he had also conducted 'area familiarization' meetings in the city.

What the fuck did that mean?

The whole thing made Misha nervous and suspicious. GRU generals didn't run around Vienna openly. It was too risky. The Americans, French, Brits, Austrians, or Germans might catch on. Not to mention the Chinese, the Iranians, or even the Israelis. But Misha couldn't say anything. He had to tread lightly. The GRU were not to be messed with—as they said, you don't fuck around with a huge, rabid, she-wolf.

Misha waited patiently and, a few weeks later, received a report that the Moscow CIA station chief—known by all as the Fat Man—had also been in Vienna during the same dates as the general. Misha did not believe in coincidences. But he had enough wisdom not to rush to judgment or to make hasty conclusions.

"Slow is smooth, and smooth is fast," went the saying. One of his teachers had even quoted Bruce Lee: "Be like water, my friend."

He would pay the General a visit, but not quite yet. Patience was a virtue.

The Apartment

The FSB, guided by Misha, had gone back to check on Yuri's apartment, only to find it empty. They checked flight manifests, border checkpoints, and train logs. Nothing. Yuri had vanished, disappeared once again. He was a ghost.

The FSB agents assigned to the case—two of Misha's best—remembered that Yuri had been Spetsnaz and GRU-trained. Such people had a certain reputation, and for good reason. New GRU recruits were forced to watch a GRU traitor being incinerated to death in a furnace. No young officer ever forgot the screams or the look on the ill-fated GRU officer's eyes as he realized what was happening and felt the warmth of the furnace and the red-hot glow of its embers.

The FSB agents returned to the office empty-handed and briefed Misha, who thanked them for their efforts. He listened carefully, wondering the entire time, *Where would Yuri go?* Had he killed himself? This was a possibility, as many traumatized veterans of the wars in Afghanistan and Chechnya had done so, including officers. But a check of hospitals, morgues, and psychiatric clinics came up empty.

The following month, Misha got a clue. The general had made a trip to Sergeyev Posad, which seemed odd. GRU generals, who were party members and atheists, tended not to visit monasteries.

A refresher check of the general's file did not reveal any religiosity. What was he doing in Sergeyev Posad?

Further investigation revealed that he had brought a care-package, including sweets, wine, cheeses, and fruits for one of the lay brothers. But nobody could recall who. Of course, the FSB could question them all, and it had a well-deserved reputation for boorishness. But Misha preferred a gentler, more patient approach. He preferred to listen and to learn slowly. But a check of monastery records revealed no lay brother or monk named Yuri or meeting his description.

That night Misha dreamt. He dreamt of Mongol hordes, of cities and villages ablaze, of children being sold into slavery, and of women being raped. He saw blood and horses lying along dirt roads, and from all sides he heard wailing and pitiful pleas to God. He heard the pounding of hooves and could smell the Mongols. Could see the fire in their eyes, taste their sweat and the oils from their pelts that covered their bodies. He heard their war cries, followed by the screaming of women and children.

But then the dream shifted. There was a blinding white light, chariots, white birch trees, and horsemen in flowing white robes, shining brilliantly. A caravan stretched endlessly, for thousands of miles, until the line turned into an empty road, much like the one in Repin's painting 'The Vladimirka,' except that this caravan had now arrived at the gates of a large, white-walled, blue-domed monastery, where the believers wept, sang, and prayed, and were met by monks who welcomed them into Earth's heavenly kingdom.

Misha cried out so loudly that he woke his wife, then burst into tears. A moment later, he realized where he was and he laughed out loud for the first time in years. His wife hugged him, comforted him, and caressed his face, wiping away his tears.

So... Yuri's in a monastery. The General is hiding him in among monks, of all things. But why?

The General and Misha

The following week, the general drove to Sergeyev Posad. He acted the tourist, walked with the crowds, and hired a guide. He took in the beauty of the onion domes, their majestic shapes and contrast with the white walls of the monastery. It was centuries old, part of the Golden Ring that had preserved Russian culture and staved off the Mongols and their cruel horde. He found it both disquieting and oddly serene.

He walked, smoked, and listened to the chanting of the monks. What he did not know, and could not know, was that the Watcher and the Jew were nearby, following him with care, to see if he'd lead them to Yuri. But unlike the general, who had an inside contact— one of the monks had been his Spetsnaz unit's chaplain—he could go where they could not. And so the general disappeared into a private part of the monastery, behind closed doors.

He wrote a message on a postcard of Solovki, one of the oldest and most remote monasteries in Russia, located hundreds of miles away, north of the Arctic Circle. The note read: "I am praying for you. Be at peace, my friend."

The general thanked his friend, who would slip the postcard to Yuri, and departed for Moscow. The Watcher and the Jew were puzzled but never saw any sign of Yuri. Perhaps the general had another agent therein, and it was all a ruse. But when walking to his car, the general had a certain spring in his step, even smiling as he got back into his vehicle.

Both the Watcher and the Jew would report this display of emotion in their coded messages to their respective headquarters.

The next morning, Yuri had disappeared. Like Francisco and Señor Lopez, he too had never really existed. God owned him now; he was a child of God.

He was never seen again.

The Seal of the Confessional

Father Ishmael was surprised when an elderly Russian-appearing man in overalls, work boots, and a cap appeared when confessions began the following Saturday. He did not recognize the man, which puzzled him, but he reminded himself that sometimes penitents would take confession at a different church.

"Bless me Father, for I have sinned."

The older man recited his sins, and Father Ishmael gave him ten Hail Marys. "Hail Mary, full of grace, the Lord is with Thee. Blessed art Thou among women, and blessed is the fruit of Thy womb, Jesus."

Then the general switched to Spanish. "Forgive my intrusion, Padre. I am a general of the GRU. You do not know me, but I know you, and I know of you. It's okay, Padre, no harm will come to you. I know of your negotiations and work with the embassy and the Nuncio. I know that you are to be part of the trade of the Russian businessman illegally held in prison for the American who claims to be a priest, along with my friend, whom the Hague seeks as a material witness. He is the one the Americans have been searching for. Rest assured, you will never find him until the trade. He is far away, somewhere safe. The details of the trade will be arranged by the CIA station chief, whom you've met and whom you know as the Fat Man, and our FSB contact, who is known to you as Misha. I will be there as well. The trade will take place in Vienna. Your people will be in touch. *Vaya con Dios, Padre.*"

He left the confessional and, once Father Ishmael had left, the church was empty. Both the Watcher and the Jew missed this one. They had each—separately—seen the general leave his office earlier that day but missed when he disappeared. When an old worker reeking of alcohol ambled past them, babbling incoherently, neither gave him a second glance.

Father Ishmael briefed the Ambassador and the Fat Man the next day. They were stunned that a GRU general would make such a risky approach, but they—especially the Fat Man—admired his creativity, inventiveness, and gumption. The Fat Man had already been contacted by Misha and the general via liaison channels. The trade was to take place the following week in Vienna, Austria, outside the main part of Schwechat Airport. The Fat Man and Misha would fly together on a Russian military jet with the released American priest, and Father Ishmael would be present at the scene, along with the Nuncio and the American Ambassador, who would travel separately.

Back in America, the Attorney General, the CIA director, and the President had been briefed on the trade. Likewise, the Vienna station chief and US Ambassador in Vienna knew the plan.

The Trade

The parties waited for hours at the outskirts of Schwechat Airport near a restricted area, all dressed in their Sunday best. It was a formal occasion. Both the Nuncio and Father Ishmael wore formal dark suits with clerical collars and black Oxfords. The Fat Man had put together a 3-piece suit with a Swiss pocket watch and his trademark yarmulke. He looked less like a spy than a diamond dealer from Antwerp. They waited patiently, along with the Ambassadors and Misha, who had worn his most formal suit displaying his medals, including his proudest one, Hero of the Russian Federation.

The Russians had dressed the American priest in his clerical suit for the flight to Vienna, and he appeared clean-shaven when he walked down the steps. He had also been examined medically by the embassy medical officer in Moscow, who'd pronounced him fit to fly. The priest had spoken little during the three-hour flight from Moscow, praying and reciting the Rosary silently.

Next, the arms dealer disembarked, likewise clean-shaven and dressed in a formal suit and looking fit and healthy as an FBI special agent escorted him to the Russian plane. But the trade wasn't over yet.

From the far corner of the runway, an official Austrian airport vehicle appeared, and out stepped the general in his finest dress uniform, festooned with all his medals, awards, and ribbons. He walked slightly ahead of Yuri and greeted Misha, the Fat Man, the Nuncio, and the Ambassadors. Due to his limp, Yuri followed the general a few steps behind until he reached the FBI special agent and a senior investigator from the Hague Tribunal, who were waiting for him.

The trade was a great success. There were smiles all around and, once all parties were airborne, toasts, cheers, and high-fives. What a glorious day! The Nuncio and Father Ishmael hugged the liberated priest, and all three wept and prayed together. Like the Prodigal Son, he had returned to them. "God is great, indeed, He is truly great."

So why was something wrong? What was missing? As a famous teacher of Father Ishmael's had once said, "We never know the complete story. There is always something missing." Nobody on the ground had seen it. But when Yuri boarded the American aircraft, he looked back at the General, and smiled.

Was it a sign? What did it mean?

The Watcher knew it right away. And so did the Jew, also surveilling the scene from his vantage point hundreds of yards away. Both saw the limp, and they knew: *Fuck*! He was favoring the wrong leg! *Yuri wasn't Yuri.* He looked like Yuri, had his features, his passport, and his other relevant documents. But he wasn't Yuri. He was somebody else. If that were the case, then where was Yuri?

When the Fat Man and the Ambassador got the report the next day, they were enraged. The Nuncio and Father Ishmael never knew the truth. They only saw God's grace in the release of the priest, who flew back to America to reunite with his family before reassignment to a Russian-speaking parish near Brighton Beach. It was a minor miracle. God's glory had shone through.

The Pushkin Museum

Misha had always enjoyed art, a holdover from his time in Berlin, with its avant-garde art scene. So he had taken a Saturday off from his usual paperwork—there were always reports to write and e-mails to wade through—to visit the Pushkin Museum, which was hosting an exhibition of Salvador Dali's art.

Misha was amazed by Dali's creative genius and energy while in equal parts repelled by Dali's sexualized perversions. There were famous paintings such as "The Spectre of Sex Appeal" and "The Great Masturbator," which highlighted Dali's outré obsessions. Misha had read that Dali had once proclaimed that the southern French city Perpignan was the center of the universe, because when he got off the train there, he had an erection in the train station. *Bozhe moi!* Misha was hardly a prude, but for him, as for most Russians, this was a bit much.

Dali preoccupied Misha's thoughts so that he didn't notice the two men following him home and into his apartment. Therefore, he never felt the sedative being injected into his neck as his legs wobbled and he sank into unconsciousness. Misha never felt himself being stripped down to his underwear and tied to a contraption with a framed print of "The Great Masturbator" on the wall next to him and a garrote around his neck. He never felt his hand around his penis, now stiff with rigor mortis, and never saw the FSB crime scene photographers or the Investigative Committee's lead investigator, who said, "What a fucking mess. What the *fuck*? Let's close it up, now. We'll tag it 'auto-erotic asphyxiation,' okay?"

And neither Misha nor the FSB and Investigative Committee investigators saw the general's unmarked car parked across the street.

Vienna

The Fat Man had contacted the general upon his return to Moscow, requesting that they meet again in Vienna. Soon after, a sunny afternoon found them sitting in the Burggarten, chatting pleasantly like two old pensioners.

"You betrayed me, General. After our understanding not to mention our assistance to your wife."

"Please, know how grateful she is, and I am, to you. You gave her life. It is a beautiful life, a life *worthy* of life! For this I can never repay you, and I thank you for returning her whole, back to me. Please know this."

"What about Yuri? You knew that the guy at the airport wasn't Yuri. He was a double. You owe me, you owe us an explanation, General."

"Ah, my friend, *moi drug*, let me explain. I am only telling you this because you are a friend."

The Fat Man's expression did not change but he inclined his head for the general to continue.

"Yuri's at peace, my friend. In the first Chechen war, and earlier, in Afghanistan, he suffered greatly. I knew him for many years and was his commanding officer in Spetsnaz, and later, when I was a GRU liaison officer in Bosnia. I brought him there to escape from the horrors of his life, his pain in Russia. Of course, this turned out to be a mistake, for we saw evil like few others…the war crimes and genocide they perpetrated against the Bosnian Muslims. Until then, like you and your American masters, we could not begin to imagine the cruelty and barbarism of the Serbs. We knew Mladić— we'd trained him, after all—and we'd seen enough of Milošević and Karadžić to know what to expect. But none could have foreseen what happened in Srebrenica. Yuri certainly did not, and it broke his spirit. He had nobody and had lost his entire family earlier. I owed it to him. Do you not take care of your own? It's part of our training in Spetsnaz. I *had* to help him, if only to ease his soul. So I relocated him to America. But that fell apart when your immigration authorities did an investigation at his work. It didn't involve Yuri, but he didn't know that. He reached out to me, and I had to bring him home. So here we are. And you can appreciate that Russia could not tolerate, or countenance, public knowledge that its military advisors were embedded with the Bosnian Serb military— much less witnesses to the horrors of Srebrenica. And I also had to worry about the FSB. They'd kill him as a nuisance. They're a bunch of thugs. Misha doesn't know what you know. It is our secret, OK? Yuri's in a far-away monastery, where he has found peace. He has taken his vows and is an ordained priest and monk. He prays daily, and is part of something bigger, part of a faith community, and part of Mother Russia. That's good enough for me. You will never find him. Russia is a huge country. Don't even try. Even your very impressive Native American tracker won't find him." The general sighed, as if exhausted by his own explanation. "Oh, I also know of your own transfer. Good luck to you. Perhaps will shall meet again. Thank you for what you have done for me, for Yuri, and more importantly, for Russia."

Daniel and the Lions

The Fat Man was so unbelievably obese that CIA's polygraph examiner couldn't get the recording device around his chest.

The poly was routine, or so the Fat Man thought. But it had been triggered by other 'anomalies,' as they were called. The polygrapher looked young. He wore a dark suit, looked like an undertaker, and never smiled. He wore no facial expression whatsoever.

"So, please tell me, Daniel, were you at the park in Vienna to recruit the Russian GRU general? Did you offer him any assistance of any kind? Did you offer him anything not sanctioned by CIA Headquarters? Did you recently, since your return from Moscow, receive a direct deposit from Erste Bank in Vienna, for the amount of $1 million?"

The Fat Man was stunned. How could the agency know of his last meeting in Vienna with the general? Had the general burned him?

"No, I was recruiting him. The meeting was sanctioned. I don't know anything about a bank transfer."

By now he was sweating, close to having a panic attack. His pulse was 130.

The examiner again asked, "Please answer the questions, yes or no. Your earlier answers showed deception."

Daniel breathed slowly and tried to find his wind. But his respiration only spiraled upward. The poly ended suddenly, and he was taken to a local ER, where tests were run and an EKG showed sinus tachycardia.

Soon after, Daniel was released and drove himself home to his apartment in Virginia. His panic hadn't really ended, for now he realized how little he knew. The Mossad, his own people, his fellow Jews, had betrayed him. They had—the fucking bastards!—sent footage of his Vienna meetings with the general to Langley.

After his failed poly, his clearance had been immediately suspended. Heedless of this, Daniel again made a desperate phone call to the general's personal phone in Moscow. He left a message: "It's me. They know. Please call me. *Please.*" He received no answer, and when he tried again, the phone had been disconnected.

The General never left a stone unturned and always made sure to tidy up loose ends. His office had wired the money to Daniel's bank account in Virginia, knowing it would get flagged by the IRS and the Agency. As a final flourish, the memo associated with the bank transfer stated, "For Services Rendered."

A few days later, the General was reading the Washington *Post* when he came across the headline: "High-ranking CIA Official Found Dead in Local Hotel Room." The article described how Daniel had been found dead from an overdose in his hotel room in downtown Washington, DC, in a state of rigor mortis, with no suicide note present. Only an empty bottle of pills next to him. The article went on to say that the CIA officer had been a high-ranking official, specializing in Russia, and that he had served in Moscow as station chief.

The General smiled and thought, *That's quite tragic.* Like Stalin had once said, "The death of one person is a tragedy, but the death of one million is a mere statistic." The Fat Man had been a superb recruit and aided the Motherland with great distinction.

For his part, the general was awaiting his transfer to a new overseas assignment as *Rezident.* He played his favorite concerto, the Rachmaninoff Second Piano Concerto, and poured himself a glass of Cabernet to celebrate.

115

Solovki

My name is Zhenya, and I am a monk at the Solovetsky Monastery. I was once somebody else—Yuri—but he is no more. Solovki is my home. Here I can pray and, yes, I've found peace. I only need think of God, and I see His face everywhere. I see Him in icons, in my fellow monks, and in the old Archimandrite, who blessed me during his visit. He had a long white beard, and the gentlest of eyes. His hands were frail, his veins thin blue lines in mottled skin. He prayed with me. He took my hands and blessed me. "Bless this young man, my Lord, and watch over him. Ease his pains and sufferings, as You did those of Jesus on the Cross. Bring him peace." I wept. "Tears are good, my son, God is good."

I take pleasure in walks along the walls of the monastery. I love its blue domes and white walls. It saved Russia and has stood the test of time for centuries. I see the flowers in the summer, and the bees, horseflies, and birds. There is joy here, there are colors. God is ever present. This is Russia.

Tourists visit here. Sometimes it's my job to guide them, to speak to them of our history. I want them to feel what I feel. But how can they? How can they, mere tourists, feel *my* life, *know* my life, know me, or know of Him? How can they know of His glory?

Once, we had an unusual tourist. He was a senior diplomat, an American, I think. I'm not sure. He wore casual loafers and a windbreaker. He liked to walk. He asked questions, lots of them. He looked like Chekhov's double, even had his countenance and gait. It was eerie. His Russian was beautiful, even poetic. He hummed and sang Russian tunes as he walked. His eyes sparkled. He wore his wedding ring on his right hand, like a Russian. So maybe I am wrong and he was only an ordinary Russian.

I took the train to Kem, following the White Sea Canal, built by Stalin using slave labor, and then flew to Archangelsk. I dreamt of thousands who died and perished in that horrible canal, and its cruel winters. I heard their screams and saw their frozen bodies in the canal and along the taiga. Once I arrived at Archangelsk, I took a small boat across the White Sea. After a few days, I arrived at Solovki, hungry, cold, but alive. So alive! I am home, at last I am home.

I have forgotten my past. It does not exist, nor does Yuri exist. There is no Grozny, no Srebrenica. The General saved me, I know this; he is a good and kind man. More than that, he is a gift from God. I have not seen him, but he is in my prayers. He too suffered and is a child of God.

I no longer dream of the past. I have forgotten my wife and child. I loved them and grieved for them, but to truly love God, I had to let them go. What moves me now is the daily Jesus Prayer: "Lord Jesus Christ, Son of God, have mercy on me."

The winters here are harsh, like Russia. Snow and icicles hang like a shroud on the monastery's walls. I can hear the snowflakes and sense the cold, oh, yes, the cold. And the long nights, with only a small halo of sunlight during those endless winter days. But then comes the joy of summer, of White Nights, and of the Aurora Borealis. In this there is glory, yes, His glory.

I am Zhenya. Yuri is no more. But I cannot always escape my past. My powers of awareness and observation are always with me. It too, is who I am. One day I was hosting a group of tourists and recounting Solovki's history. Many asked questions and wanted photos with me. That's fine too. But one was odd and didn't speak.

He was young, with dark, piercing eyes. His skin was reddish-brown, and he looked like an Uzbek or a Mongol. He was silent, and never said a word during the tour. He took no photos either. But at the end of the tour, he took my hands in his, and smiled, saying, "Thank you Yuri, for this special day. I am glad that you have found peace here." His Russian was perfect, beautiful. When I looked up, he had vanished.

A Jew in Belgrade

The Mossad spy had left the Hague shortly after the failed trade in Vienna. But his masters had rewarded him with a posting in Belgrade as chief of its Mossad office. For the first time in many years, he found himself back home, in a place of his childhood memory. At long last he could take in Serbia, its people, its smells, and its food. He'd walk for hours along the side streets of Skadarlija, where he could stop for a plate of *cevapćići*—pork sausages—and a Serbian salad. He craved a taste of *burek* pastry in the morning with a Turkish coffee.

As a child, his family's maid—a gypsy—would tell their fortunes in Serbian by reading the grains of coffee overturned in the tiny cup's saucer. She had jet-black hair and several gold teeth. She smiled often. But when she read his fortune, she said, "You will travel far and wide, and you will be alone. You will see many things—wars, crimes, massacres, and evil. Be careful, my boy."

Once more he could talk walk to and pray at Belgrade's famous synagogue, Sukat Shalom, built in the 1920s. There he could recite the Kaddish for the dead, and he could hear the cries and laughter of the departed. He knew the community's history, dating back several centuries, when a colony of Sephardic Jews settled along the banks of the Sava. Moshe knew these things. He also knew of his namesake, Moshe Pijade, one of Tito's closest and earliest Partisan leaders during WWII, and later the first President of Yugoslavia.

Moshe was undeclared, so he had to watch his back, lest he become a target of the efficient, aggressive Serbian counterintelligence services. So he acted like no one. Just an ordinary Jewish guy, like a tourist. He walked in old Belgrade, where he could stop and enjoy a coffee, and then proceed to Kalemegdan Park and its historic castle, partaking of a fine meal and drinks overlooking the river.

He visited the city's art museums and their fantastical, magical realist, naïve art. There were paintings of dogs, wolves, peasants, and chickens. Moshe recoiled at the horrific, nationalist, blood-soaked paintings of Milić od Maćve, highlighting nationalist war criminals in Bosnia blessing the 'heroes and martyrs.'

At home, alone, he read poetry, especially the eerie poems of Vasko Popa, with wolves howling, suckling their young, and emerging from darkness. This too was Serbia.

Sometimes he wondered, *Where is Yuri? What about the General? The Fat Man? And what of Father Ishmael?* How their lives had intertwined. They were all wanderers and searchers, yearning for justice and for peace. What did they find?

The Mossad knew many things, and Moshe knew its history, his history, and Israel's history. He also knew Serbia intimately, including its recent history of unthinkable war crimes in Bosnia and Kosovo. Moshe struggled to make sense of this. He loved Serbia and the Serbs, but he hated that other part of it. And yet it was his suffering to bear. He had recruited agents who had served in the various paramilitary groups, such as Arkan's Tigers, and he had recruited other agents from the Serbian secret services who had supported and funded such bloody escapades.

Moshe said to himself, *I am a Jew, I am Israeli, and I am a Serb. I am three persons in one, a trinitarian existence. What does that mean, and where can I find peace? Did Yuri find peace? What about Father Ishmael?*

One Passover, he stopped by the old synagogue and stepped inside. He prayed with the Holy Assembly and sang songs of Exodus. He ate the unleavened bread. As he left, he found himself weeping, as if performing some kind of self-cleansing. Weeping for all his peoples, the Jews and the Serbs, for Israel, Serbia, and most of all, for Srebrenica, for his Muslim brothers and sisters, for their loss, His loss, and humanity's loss. Never again.

Diné

The Watcher had never failed on a mission. He had been following the general for the past year or more, and he had succeeded
beyond the agency's wildest expectations. Now with the trade over,
he was slated to transfer back to America for additional training.
Before leaving, though, he had one more surveillance run to complete: tracing the general's movements to Vienna, as he had recently
learned of the general's upcoming transfer.

It was supposed to be easy, a mere formality. The general was
on his way to the Foreign Ministry for a briefing with the new
Ambassador to Austria. It was a gorgeous clear day, and the old
commander had stopped along the Arbat for a coffee. So, the
Watcher did likewise.

The Watcher was wearing slacks and a sport coat, as he had
come straight from teaching. He looked like any other businessman or well-heeled tourist on the Arbat. When the general got up
to leave, the Watcher paid for his coffee as well. As he stood, he felt
the gun at his ribs.

"Please, won't you join us for a ride, sir? The general would like
to chat with you."

He got in the car, which was an elegant, German-made vehicle
with tinted windows. He didn't know what would come next. The
driver and the general's bodyguards were silent, not a word spoken.

An hour later, he found himself at a lovely *dacha* on the outskirts of Moscow. The air smelled of birches and firs, and the general's garden was vibrant with blooming flowers and mushrooms.

By the time his captors led him to the front door of the house, the general was already inside.

"Hello, my friend," he told the Watcher. "We meet at last. It's a pleasure. Welcome to my *dacha*, our family's summer home. Would you care to join me in picking mushrooms, or would you rather chat over tea?"

The Watcher replied, "Thank you. Tea would be fine."

So they sat outside near the garden, admiring the flowers, listening to birds chirping, their songs underlain by the babbling of a nearby brook. The general served tea with bread and herring, *zakuski*. He spoke first.

"I know of your work, and I admire your skills. Tell me about yourself, as your gifts are very special. Please don't be evasive. Just tell me who you are. Nobody has *ever* been able to get this close to me before. So you must be very special. I want to understand you. Do not be afraid. If I wanted to kill you, it would have already happened. Please, tell me more about yourself."

The Watcher nodded. "Have you seen the movie *Derzu Uzala*? I'm like that. I'm a Navajo; I grew up on the land, on a reservation in Arizona. My father taught me to track at a very young age. He was a shaman as well, just like Derzu Uzala. He taught me that the wilderness was made by the Creator, and it was too vast to comprehend. Just as Captain Arseniev said to Derzu Uzala, 'Man is too small to understand the vastness of nature.' And so it is with Russia. I love its expansiveness and its natural beauty. My assignment is coming to an end, general, and I will weep when I leave, just as I wept when I finished hiking the Grand Canyon, over many months and hundreds of miles. Russia has touched me deeply. Solovki reminded me of that, but in a different way. It is ice, not fire. It is snow, and I loved its emptiness. You did well to place Yuri there. He is at peace, general."

"How did you know to find him there? I never went there, nor did any other Russian officials. Nothing was written down or even spoken. Please tell me how you knew this."

Despite the tense situation, the Watcher smiled and shrugged. "Sometimes knowing is in the heart. As a child, my father and my grandfather taught me to trust my heart and my instincts. I had to think, not just like you, although your idea of placing Yuri at Solovki was brilliant, but to also enter into Yuri's soul. I had to become Yuri, I had to embrace his suffering, and I had to understand: If I were Yuri, where in Russia could I find peace? I crossed the White Sea on a small fishing boat. When I saw the island, I understood as you did that Yuri's mission was over. He was free. And I too could be free. What *is* freedom, General? Surely, you've also thought of such matters. When I saw Yuri, and looked in his eyes, I felt happiness. When I left Solovki, I wept with joy. It was my farewell to Russia. Now I can go home, general. Of course, like you, I will have new assignments, other missions. But no place can ever touch me as this beautiful country has done. And yet as the great French alpinist Maurice Herzog said, There are other Annapurnas in the lives of men. Goodbye general, and as they say in Russian, *s Bogom*."

The general sipped his tea and smiled. His heart fluttered a bit at hearing this young Navajo's stirring words. He thought of Yuri and saw this young man in him. He got up, embraced the Watcher, and said, "Goodbye my friend. I shall miss you."

He got in his vehicle told his bodyguards to drive him to the Foreign Ministry. This mission, too, was finally over. He had done his part, and new missions, new challenges, awaited him. The general smiled, remembering the ethos of his Spetsnaz unit—*sila, smirenje, i smelost*. Strength, humility, and courage. Tomorrow was a new day.

Lunch with the General

The embassy psychiatrist in Moscow had also moved on to his next posting—in Vienna. It was a comfortable, delightful posting in a city of a million or so, with historic parks, fresh air, culture, good schools, amenities, and a high quality of life. And his region—eastern Europe and the Balkans— lay close-by and largely free of crises, dramas, or emergencies. If anything, compared to Moscow, it was somewhat boring. But the embassy psychiatrist had had experienced plenty of drama, crises, and emergencies during his years in Moscow, not to mention his assignments throughout central Asia.

Or so he thought.

One day, he was walking home, now dressed in his usual suit (the embassy in Vienna was a more formal sort of place), when an elegant car with Russian diplomatic plates pulled up.

The driver opened the door and called out, "Please get in, Doctor. Your visit is expected by the Russian Ambassador."

He did so and, after a few minutes, arrived at the Russian Ambassador's residence. It was an ornate, historic building. He was greeted by the Ambassador's staff aide, who greeted and thanked him in perfect English. "The Ambassador is aware of your busy schedule and wanted to have lunch with you. This is a rare honor, and one that he grants to very few foreign diplomats. Unfortunately, he has a meeting at the foreign ministry and won't be able to be here. But he has asked another guest to take his place and to make you feel welcome. While you're waiting, may I offer you a drink? Coffee? Tea? A glass of wine, perhaps? Will you be working later this afternoon?"

The psychiatrist was at a loss for words and didn't quite know what to say. "Thank you, just a glass of water and a coffee, please."

So he could barely contain his shock when the general and his wife entered the waiting room.

"Doctor, so lovely to see you. Thank you for coming. My wife" —she shook his hand and kissed his cheeks *bussi bussi*, Austrian style—and I are honored to host you for lunch. Yes, to anticipate your question, we're now stationed here, where I am the GRU *Rezident*. A reward for my labors and service to the Motherland, I suppose. But enough diplomatic gossip, let us talk of happier things. We wish to, first of all, thank you for what you have done for my beloved wife, for me, and for our family. And my country thanks you for your service. You gave her—and us—our life back. We are indebted to you and deeply grateful. *Spasibo*, Doctor."

And so they spoke, not of diplomacy or espionage, but of simpler things. Of their travels, families, cultural offerings in Vienna, and of life's joys and wonders. They spoke of their children, of growing old, and of finding a little bit of peace and *gemutlichkeit* in Vienna. The general's wife—her name was Nina—looked radiant as she graciously served blini, herring, black bread, borscht soup, salad, and coffee. They drank toasts to each other and to their families. The couple asked about his family, his wife, and his children.

Finally, they presented the doctor with a gift, a signed, first edition version of Chekhov's memoirs.

"Chekhov was a doctor too, you know that, right, Doctor? Do you write?"

It was a splendid afternoon. Finally, before they parted, the general smiled and said, "Doctor, as you can see, your gifts have not escaped me. With the permission of both our and your ambassador, we may occasionally request assistance from you. Oh, don't worry: I've already discussed this with them. They are most pleased and in awe of your skills. We know how you helped your ambassador's manic-depressive, adolescent daughter become well. She is now a happy, well-adjusted young lady and doing well in school. Don't act shocked, Doctor. I know that you believe that Vienna is a city of secrets and that the unconscious is alive and well here. Of course! It is the city of Freud, correct? But please remember, there *are* no secrets in Vienna. Goodbye, Doctor, perhaps we shall meet again."

Millenium Challenge

Father Ishmael returned to a quieter life, one of normalcy, prayer, routine, and solitude. The Ambassador had finished his assignment and moved back to the US. The Fat Man had also completed his tour and returned to a senior posting at headquarters before his untimely, tragic death. Now, Father Ishmael found himself enjoying Moscow's simpler pleasures, and there was so much to explore.

He found himself enthralled by the Novodevichy Monastery, especially in winter, savoring its snow-lined trees and domes. He sought out its peace and serenity, particularly its candle-lit interiors. He lit a candle for Francisco and his family, for the Ambassador, and for the Fat Man. He had kept in touch with the priest who had returned to America after his release from Lefortovo. His had become a calm, serene existence.

Father Ishmael prayed his Rosary daily, and its daily recitations brought peace and solace. He finally found himself freed of his sorrows. He dreamt not of death and casualty but of joy. This showed in his homilies, which tended toward the hopeful. He spoke of God's many blessings and reminded his flock, "Jesus is always with us."

Father Ismael saw beauty everywhere. He saw a ballet performance of Swan Lake at the Bolshoi, and afterward, savored a drink at the café in the Hotel Metropol and took in its elegance. It was a truly great hotel, which had hosted presidents, prime ministers, diplomats, and spies. He admired its chandeliers and its old-world charm.

And how could he forget Moscow's great museums, such as the Tretyakov, with its paintings by Repin, Kuznetsov, and others. He couldn't get enough of the Alexander Gardens, their tulips radiant in spring. And the bulky majesty of the Kremlin—what not to embrace about its stately wonder? And then there was the Chekhov Museum. His guides were two elderly ladies who spoke fondly of Chekhov, as if they had known him. They told him that to understand Chekhov, you must go outside of Moscow. To understand the real Russia, one had to take leave of Moscow's excesses.

Moscow was brand-name luxury shops, $200-per-table restaurants, luxury automobiles, and the indescribable wealth of the new businessmen, the Russian Mafia, their summer homes on the Riviera, dachas springing up like wildflowers in the countryside, drinks at the Red Bar—fully decked out in gorgeous red leather, with red-leather mini-skirted waitresses in red Gucci shoes.... The entire spectrum of Moscow's assaults upon the senses seemed oddly familiar. But underneath it all, to glimpse the 'real' Russia, one only had to drive 10 miles beyond the MKAD ring road to a small *izba*, and there one would find rooks in spring, groves of white birches, a peasant riding his bicycle to market, and a small church. There, Chekhov's double would be waiting, sitting in his study at Melikhovo, writing of the travails of his journeys to Sakhalin, wiping his brow and his fogged-up glasses, remembering his passions with a local tart, never too far from his spittoon, its collection of bloody mucous and spittle belying the tubercular illness that would eventually claim the writer.

1999. Father Ishmael could not imagine the future, nor could his flock, or even his fellow Russian citizens. He would not have been surprised by its 'loss' of the Cold War; it represented a moral war which the USSR could never hope to win. But he too would have later understood Russia's rise back, led by a young, determined ex-KGB officer, whose steely eyes and countenance projected not only firm strength, but quintessential Russianness, his cold humility combined with unyielding discipline, honed by his years of practice in Judo and Sambo. The new leader had grown up in the ashes of Leningrad, its brutal siege the unspoken stuff of dinner-table conversations with his war-wearied parents. He had grown up a weakling, easily beaten on the playgrounds and preyed upon by hooligans, hence his later journey into the martial arts. He would study the language of the enemy, Germany, and would learn to love and respect it when, later, he became President. The new leader's Russia would once again be strong and respected and would give no quarter. The world would learn that Russia would not countenance humiliation; that it would never again be beaten.

Perhaps Father Ishmael would have later understood Russia's compelling need to destroy the Chechen terrorists—"cockroaches" is what the Russian President called them—who later brought their hatreds and bloodlust to Moscow's Nord-Ost Theater and to a small school in Beslan. Father Ishmael would have understood Russia's need to regain her strength—a survival imperative. Had he been there, he would have intuited that eerie sense at Nord-Ost and Beslan—just before the assaults began—that something was dreadfully wrong and it would all soon come to its terrible denouement; he too would have sensed the tension, that odd smell and mix of sweat, cigarette smoke, and cordite, as the Russian special-operations units prepared for their tragic assaults.

One day Father Ishmael received a phone call inviting him to come to the embassy to meet the new Ambassador. But Father Ishmael was in for a surprise, for he was escorted not to the Ambassador's office, but to the new station chief's office.

Epiphany

The new station chief was tall and wore a formal suit. He smiled easily and had had blue eyes and blond hair.

"*Buenos dias, Padre.* Or *mir tesen,* as they say in Russian."

The easy familiarity shocked Father Ishmael, as diplomats were usually a bit more formal and stuffy. He didn't recognize the gentleman standing in front of him.

"May I offer you a coffee and some tea cakes? Make yourself comfortable, Father Ishmael."

The voice sounded oddly familiar, but Father Ishmael couldn't place it either. And then it clicked, and the tears began to flow. Looking into the station chief's eyes, he *knew*. It was partly the voice, the timbre, the easy charm, and the laugh. Even plastic surgery couldn't change that.

He hugged Francisco, weeping openly. "You're alive, it's really you. Praise God, Francisco! Jesus is great, God is good."

"No, Padre, you're mistaken. I am not Francisco. He died, remember? You attended his funeral. He has a star carved on the Wall of Honor at agency headquarters. You were there at the ceremony, remember? There is no Francisco. He's dead and gone. But I am here," he said, his eyes twinkling. He laughed easily. "Let's have a drink, *una bebida.* My name is Frank—that's my real name. And I have a story to tell you.

"I had received very serious death threats in Mexico. The cartel and its leader—El Viejo—were threatening me and my family. Oh, don't fret or worry. They're safe and living here with me. My child is in middle school and doing well. My wife works at the embassy as an administrative officer. Anyway, the agency had to exfiltrate us quickly. And they had to be creative. We needed to die in order to live. Just like our god Jesus, right? We went back to America, where the agency re-created us. I went to graduate school and language school. A long year of Russian at Middlebury, in Vermont. Then a year at headquarters to prepare for this assignment. So here I am. It's wonderful to see you, Padre."

"What about Señor Lopez?"

"Oh, don't worry. He too was relocated. He was working for us all along. He went back to graduate school like I did, got his MBA, and is now a successful venture capitalist. He had plastic surgery. You wouldn't recognize him. He's doing well and enjoying investing in technology startups in Latin America. For obvious reasons, he avoids Mexico. He sends you his best. He liked you a lot, and said that you are a genuine person, a real *hombre*, and a man of many gifts. So here we are! *Salud*, Padre!"

They embraced, prayed the Rosary together, and then Father Ismael departed. As he walked to the embassy's main gate, he smiled and saluted the flag, tears still streaming down his cheeks.

My Name is Ishmael

After Moscow, I asked to be reassigned. The Nuncio acquiesced and offered me my old parish back in Mexico City. I was assigned as an ordinary priest but also given a diplomatic passport as an apostolic delegate at large. Driving to Mexico City after a few months of leave in Texas, I reveled in Mexico's familiar magic and beauty. I was amazed by the cactus forests in the northern Chihuahan Desert. I stopped in San Miguel de Allende, where I felt grateful to hear Spanish again and absorbed the colors, smells, and the noises of the local market. It was pure joy to sit quietly, praying in its great gothic cathedral. The streets were full of shops, tourists, and artists. At night, how I loved sitting in the square and listening to the *mariachis* while drinking a *cerveza*. God is good. *"Jesus, siempre estas con migo."*

The parish felt like home. My flock had changed, but they welcomed me, and I embraced their love and gratitude. It was good to be back. I preached, I spoke of Jesus's love and His miracles on our behalf. I spoke in parables, and I spoke of Proverbs, and we recited the Psalms together. The Lord is my shepherd, I shall not want. My flock was as before, a group of expats.

I had my other calling. Every few months, the Nuncio would pay me a visit, and we drank coffee and prayed together, giving thanks to our Lord, our God. He understood, knew of, the other part of me, the negotiator, el Negociador. That too, is part of who I am. The kidnappings in Mexico never ended. And I helped where I could. There were many cases. I saw their faces in my dreams and remembrances. I saw their eyes. For me, each case was personal. The child missing, the businessman with his finger cut off, and the Jesuit priest who vanished after a trip to the mountains outside Oaxaca. That too, was my fate. One cannot fight one's fate or one's calling. We are all here to serve God, with our time, treasure, and talents.

I solved cases in many ways. Sometimes I spoke directly to the kidnappers by phone. In other cases, I never knew or met with them. Other meetings were in-person. One I will never forget. She was a vivacious, middle-aged woman with a silky voice. She sounded husky, like a Mexican Lauren Bacall. She had no fear. She invited me to negotiate at her home in San Angel. It was gorgeous, as was she. She was voluptuous and would greet me dressed in a bikini and a sexy bathrobe. I could see her cleavage, even her nipples, and her perfume was subtle. The effect was aphrodisiac. We would sit in her courtyard while sipping drinks, a kind of seduction. She would lick her lips and run her hand through her beautifully made-up hair.

When she saw my face flushing with arousal, she asked, "Have you ever thought of loving again? Do you not long for an embrace, a tender kiss, and the passions of *un amor*? Don't worry Padre, it's our secret."

Her charms and beauty masked her attraction to violence and cruelty. I knew that she would not hesitate to kill me if she felt betrayed in a negotiation.

And then there was the rancher, who lived several hours away. He ran a huge smuggling and human trafficking ring outside of Queretaro. He refused to negotiate over the phone. He told me, "To trust a man, I have to look him in the eyes." I would be taken to Queretaro, blindfolded, and then transported for two days—by burro! —to his *finca* in a remote part of the province.

He even had a small chapel on the ranch. There, he'd make me pray the Rosary with him before and after any negotiations, and he'd have me take his confession. He had a dark complexion and always wore jeans, a *guayabera*, Nocona ropers, and a black Stetson cowboy hat, all reminders of his time working as a ranch hand in Texas. He would only negotiate while drinking mescal. We took many shots, between us. He would smoke Marlboros, pinching the cigarette between his thumb and index finger. The effect was contemplative. He was both cruel and a man of honor. He never reneged on a deal.

There was much I did not understand. I never knew why these kidnappers trusted me. I told them, "*Por que negocia con migo? No soy professional. Soy solamente un padre.*" They laughed when I told them my first words in Spanish: "*El burro sabe mas que tu.*" I am only an ordinary priest, *un hombre mas comun*.

Several months later, I was on leave, visiting family in Texas. I had not been home in years. My family had moved to Dallas. It was a joyous reunion. My mother looked more beautiful than ever, and she embraced me with tears streaming down her face, saying, "It's so wonderful to see you, Ishmael."

My father looked elegant as always, wearing a three-piece suit and a Panama hat. We ate at a local, family-run Mexican seafood restaurant on the patio, enjoying cervezas and listening to the mariachis sing "*Tu, Solo Tu.*" God is great, God is good. Indeed, He is the greatest, *nuestro Salvador*.

I was sitting at a café in Dallas the next day when a distinguished gentleman of mature years, wearing a suit with a wine-colored pocket handkerchief and a pink tie sat at my table. I immediately guessed who he was.

"*Buenos Dias, Señor Lopez. Que buena onda!* So good to see you."

"Hello, Padre, it's been a long time." Señor Lopez and I embraced, *un abrazo*. "My heart's right here, *sabes*?"

We spoke at length, and he told me his story. He too had found solace and joy. He missed and longed for Mexico. But he had found a new life in the U.S. with his wife, children, and grandchildren.

He traveled often, mostly to Latin America. Life was good. "God is good, Padre."

These tales are true, and I, like Ishmael of old, am the inheritor of this larger tale and its lost world. For they are known to me in my dreams and remembrances. I am a priest, a negotiator, a diplomat, and a lover of cultures, travel, politics, and language. I continue to walk in the footsteps of those many giants who walked before me. I can hear the voices of my forebears, prodding me on with their love of far-away lands and cultures; I can hear the call of my language teachers, urging me on, to recite the poems of Paz, Neruda, and Vallejo. And so it goes. I can see their faces, and I can hear their voices. I am transported, once again, to far-away dreams, imaginations, and wanderings. As the great poet-diplomat Octavio Paz wrote, "The river turns, moves on, doubles back, and comes full circle: it is unending and forever arriving." I too can fly, and I can dream of water, of rivers and oceans – and I can dream of journeys, of unfinished travels to far-away lands, where I can at long last hear songs of beauty, lamentation, and sorrow. And most of all, I hear His voice. Every day brings joy. I am alive, I am here, and He is always by my side.

Texas Rangers

Father Ishmael dreamt again. Before he could dream of joy, he had to dream of the past. Only then could he begin to understand it and find hope. He had to know himself. His dreams preceded his faith, even as he later learned to walk by faith, not by sight. He dreamt of his ancestors. He dreamt of settlements in Texas, of cabins along the Brazos River. He saw a white man, alone, in the stillness of the morning, canoeing down the Brazos. Who was he? Why him? The waters were shallow and gentle; *still waters run deep*, his father had told him as a boy. He dreamt of wandering. He crossed the Rio Grande, the Great River. He saw mountains, and the glow of a sunset along the Santa Elena canyon in Big Bend. He gasped and saw more. There were caves with petroglyphs and arrowheads. He saw how God created Palo Duro Canyon. Animals came to him: mountain lions, wolves, deer, armadillos, coyotes, javelinas, and wild horses. He could smell their scent. They spoke to him, and he to them. He was back in Eden. The deserts were green and lush, full of life's wonders. But then it all changed. The colors became orange and red, colors of fire and blood. He witnessed burning prairie fires, set by Comanches. Cabins burning, scalps nailed to trees, and a long eagle feather, floating in the breeze after the slaughter. There were mutilations—breasts, genitals, abdomens, necks, hearts, and brains all about. The Comanches had fled.

A Texas Ranger—one of his relatives who had ridden with them after the Civil War—told him on the battlefield, "To defeat them, we must become them. You will eat them—their hearts, livers, kidneys, and brains. You will kill their women and children. You must do this. Please understand me. We are all the same." The Ranger rode off, into the last of the canyons, alone in the sunset and its bright, fiery, blood-red glow. But his voice lingered:

"Ishmael, this is who you are. Do not try to be another. That only leads to sorrow and hurt. Be who you are, be who *we* are. There is no God here. Just man. Survive, be alive, and live to tell the story. Only the story matters. Go on, tell the tale. Goodbye, my son."

Father Ismael woke up howling and screaming, his nightshirt soaked with tears, and his body shaking for hours. He could smell the burning of bodies, cabins, trees, and prairies, and he could smell the dust, the horses, the wounded, and the dead. He longed to be held and murmured aloud, "My Lord, how I have longed for a human touch—from my Comforter and Redeemer."

Ishmael extended a hand and saw an apparition, an angel of sorts. The angel was smiling and had a gentle, comforting presence amid the whiteness surrounding it. But when Ishmael looked up, the angel had vanished.

Silence

Father Ishmael went to the confessional and spoke the words: "Bless me Father, for I have sinned."

But he stopped there, unable to continue, and simply sat and wept. He felt a mix of emotions that confused him. Joy, but also sadness. What about Jesus? Where was He? Ishmael wondered about silence. What did it mean?

He recalled the CIA agent Ambrose's statement: "Our weapons are silence and money."

Father Ishmael wondered about Yuri. What had ever happened to him? He thought of the kidnap victims he'd helped and whom he continued to assist. *Why me, Lord?* And then—*Send me, Lord.* He longed for his burden to be lifted.

Where were Marisa and her daughter, his child? Had the Lord forgotten them, as he, Ishmael, had?

The words of Shusaku Endo came to him: "Lord, I resented Your silence." To which God answered, "I was not silent. I suffered beside you."

But where are you now, *Lord?* Ishmael felt, like the priest in Endo's novel, terribly alone at times, as if he were the last priest in the land. But he knew that the Lord didn't stay silent. He had spoken many times, over and over.

Finally, Ishmael spoke to his confessor, borrowing from Endo's words: "Even if He had been silent, my life until this day would speak of Him, and I will always serve Him. For I am just a priest—an ordinary, humble priest."

Acknowledgments

Kenneth Dekleva is a practicing psychiatrist in Dallas, Texas, who previously served as a physician-diplomat with the US government, mostly overseas, including Moscow, Mexico City, New Delhi, Vienna, and London. This is his first novel. He thanks his editor Ed Stackler, the design staff at Integrative Ink, and his first readers: James Lawler, David Charney, JR Seeger, David Percelay, James Hawes, Paul Vidich, Sandie Bostick, Daniel Levin, Graham Fuller, Christopher Turner, Robert Carlin, Richard Wirick, and James Stejskal. And lastly, this novel is dedicated to his wife, daughter, and grandchildren.

Made in United States
North Haven, CT
09 February 2023

32302431R00085